Becoming Zhivago

BECOMING ZHIVAGO

Jess Wagner, MD

PALMETTO
PUBLISHING

Charleston, SC
www.PalmettoPublishing.com

Becoming Zhivago

First Edition

Paperback ISBN: 979-8-8229-0468-2

eBook ISBN: 979-8-8229-0469-9

"I am not here to exert the will of a misguided electorate, I am here to lead you to your rightful inheritance...a free and just country."

A Republican Senator who did not exist in 2020

"Fear has focused a generation, the virus has brought the world together in a confused commonality."

A Concerned Citizen in 2020

"Count no man happy until he is dead, free of pain at last."

Sophocles, Fifth Century, BC

SECTION ONE

Introduction

BECOMING ZHIVAGO IS A lifelong endeavor.

Of course, Yuri Zhivago, Doctor of Medicine, poet and fictional character is impossible to actually become. He was never real in the first place. Not real in a material sense anyway.

It is true that he *seems* to be as real to me as any other person who ever lived. Yet he was, after all, a character in a book. Or if you prefer, a man named Omar Sharif in a movie. Whether the subject lives in reality or in the imagination, it really doesn't matter. It remains impossible for anyone to ever become someone else. We are all destined to walk in our own skin, to be filled with the spirit that manifests within us. Be that a blessing or a curse.

No, it is the *process* of becoming Zhivago that is the crux of what I want to describe to you.

It is not a roadmap to sainthood. Far from it. Rather it is the pursuit of Zhivago's sensibility...his natural inclination to embrace hope and love even when confronted with the most terrible degradation and suffering. His fervent belief that blossoms will arise from the ashes because they have a natural drive to erupt. That through cycling seasons, if you must endure the bleakest of winters it is with patient eyes that you await the reemergent glory of Spring. And despite all the sorrows and wounds that may have afflicted you in the course of your journey, your character can still resist the corruption of your soul.

I am not ashamed to enshrine the power of hope. I admire the courage and the heart that can so delicately focus tenderness in the fury of a tempest. To care for the sick while fires are raging all around. To be driven by the love of a woman through the harshest of winter storms to find her and rejoin her. I have made it my ambition to try and view the world through such a lens. From a spiritual overflowing such as this poetry can surely emerge. Poems that crystalize the experience of living with wide open eyes in a world of great joy and great sorrow.

Becoming Zhivago seems a fine metaphor for the path I wish to follow.

CHAPTER 1

Saint Helena Island

I ENTERED THIS LIFE four years after Adolph Hitler put a bullet in his deranged brain. This was an excellent cosmic break since I was born in the USA, the land of unmolested industrial plants and the booming expansion of middle-class opportunities. I say this not to glorify my times, there are endless faults to assign to this age. Rather, I say this to contrast my experience with the horrific challenges of my parent's generation.

I'd like to tell you what it felt like to live in the bubble of the second half of the twentieth century and, thank the Lord, to be still going into the twenty first. It was a unique time and I predict generations to come will reflect upon these days with envy and wonder.

I would like to start my narrative not near the beginning of this span of years but much closer to the present.

I'll begin about 18 months ago, the summer of 2019:

I was thinking about Yuri Zhivago the first time we pulled up to take a look at our place on Saint Helena Island, South Carolina. I truly admired him as if I had known him in life. To me he is a tragic yet heroic figure. There had been nights over the years, I'll confess, when I would try to commune with his spirit. It was a one-way conversation of course, but I always felt better for the time I spent trying.

He had overcome witnessing wholesale human slaughter, the total upheaval of his family and his society. He had suffered the most punishing physical deprivations and surviving all of that, he had still managed to preserve the capacity to love and to celebrate the beauty of life itself.

If you haven't seen the movie or read the book you are really missing something brilliant and beautiful. Boris Pasternak won the Nobel prize largely because of this novel.

I flashed on the absurdity of comparing my life to his. The comfort and ease I had endured on my way to the age of 70 could not remotely be compared to Zhivago's trials and suffering. My life was hardly a frigid limp across the Russian steppe in winter with a slender hope of survival. So far, my travail had been a series of safe passages past surmountable obstacles. In fact, I had been cast upon the shore of existence at a golden time, a span of unprecedented personal freedom and comfort....at least for many.

But I digress,

I was saying that my wife Lisa and I had come that day to look over a place that was on the market. It had five acres with a beautiful and snug hand-crafted log cabin that occupied a gorgeous site in the center of the property. The home was small but perfect for two. The loft and high ceilings, the many windows and glass doors gave it an expanded impression.

There were two gas fireplaces and a wood stove. The cabin had that one-of-a-kind craftsmanship that only an artist could provide, special touches everywhere. Indeed, the builder was truly an artist whose carved works hung on the walls of some of the finest local restaurants. There was not a trace of sheetrock and we fell in love with all the wood around us.

Stately live oaks draped with elegant hanging Spanish moss, majestic blooming magnolias and fruit trees graced the lush green grass and the profusion of flowering vegetation. This was surrounded on all sides by a cathedral of innumerable tall green pines that formed an unbroken canopy in every direction. There was even a large wooden deck with wooden railings that led from the bedroom to the above ground circular swimming pool in the back of the house. That would certainly come in handy during the torrid South Carolina summer heat.

The driveway was nearly invisible from the main road that ran through the center of Saint Helena Island. It was a narrow track that was little more than a stone covered trail. It passed through an acre and a half of forest weaving back and forth so that the road was no longer visible from the cleared homesite. Indeed, you could barely see where to turn onto the little lane when coming off the main road. I must admit, the thought that no one guessing a house was there really appealed to me.

Behind the cleared center acre were another acre and a half of nearly impenetrable forest. No outside structures were visible anywhere from the property. The setting gave a sense of complete privacy and isolation. This was an opportunity that Lisa and I had always talked about but had never realized. There were pens for our future chickens and parrots. A goat might be nice if it didn't eat our garden. We saw that special look in each other's eyes, that bright, happy, wonderful look that communicates in seconds what might

5

take hours to hash out in words and reasons. We put in a bid right then and there.

As luck would have it, our offer was accepted.

The first day we got the keys we drove right over. I stopped to unlock the gate at the border of the center acre. There sat the log cabin on the cleared land with its lush vegetation. Looking around I once again thought of Yuri and laughed to myself. My troika was a Honda Accord, the snows had melted into palmetto palms that were bathed in subtropical sun.

I could imagine pondering life in such splendid isolation, my beloved Lisa always by my side. I would write life affirming poems and prose immersed in these beautiful and peaceful bucolic surroundings. I would strive to exude gentle kindness, as often as I could muster it. Lisa would make the land bloom even more vibrantly than the garden spot it was on that first day that we saw it. My kids and grandkids were close by. Life was good.

Time passed tranquilly. I did not know then that this land would become an island of safety in a burning sea. I had not yet seen this ground as a Walden Pond or as a slice of Eden where I would need to clarify and even redefine my life.

No one had ever heard of Covid 19.

Though my medical specialty was Family Practice, I had just finished a stint working as an Internist around Lake Norman in southern North Carolina. If you have never been to that area, I would recommend that you to see it sometime. It lies just north of Charlotte. The countryside is lovely and the people I encountered there always seemed optimistic, friendly and helpful. Patients and the medical staff were thankful and their confidence in me was gratifying.

I had been on this end of a stethoscope for 40 years. Sometimes I reflected on the fact that it was the same length of time that Moses had spent in the desert. I would not suppose to make a personal comparison with that event. I am pointing this out because it is a long time for things to happen, to transform.

As a Family Practitioner I was well trained in Internal Medicine but also had to master the art of Pediatrics and parts and parcels of all the other medical specialties. Psychiatric training had proved to be invaluable.

At this stage in my career, I was working at practices that had temporary needs. I would travel to towns in North Carolina, South Carolina and Florida, states in which I held medical licenses. Lisa and I would stay in a residential hotel, or apartments for the longer assignments sometimes lasting many months. So it was with great relief that we found our haven on Saint Helena. We moved in during mid-August of 2019. It felt like home.

CHAPTER 2

Lisa

Now BEFORE WE GO further, I want to give you some personal history. After all, none of us comes out of a vacuum. I'll begin with a tidbit, a chance encounter that forever shaped my life. I had been out of medical school for 3 years, just finishing my residency on Long Island (Long Guy Land as it sounded to my ear). It was late June 1979 and June 30th would be the last day of my specialty training at South Side Hospital.

Bay Shore was a relatively quiet seaside town in the suburban reaches of Nassau County before it faded into the rural branches of the North and South Forks.... long before it arrived at the mansions of the Hamptons at the far east end. I was happy to be leaving and to finally pursue my destiny. Where was I headed? Out West, of course.

I had a pocket full of medical licenses and a lifetime to figure it out. California, Colorado, Oregon and Hawaii were all on my list to explore. I was single and filled with natural impulses. One day I wandered over to an administrative office that I had never been in before. I was killing time. I found a fellow resident and a junior administrator sitting in one of the rooms shooting the shit. They were lively guys, so I sat down in a chair, and they continued to chat.

"Yeah, I know what you mean," said one to the other, "I do it too. I'm getting real good at it. I'm sitting at a bar talking to some pretty young thing and with my left hand in my pocket I'm working my wedding ring off my finger."

Both of them chuckled a bit.

I will admit I was mildly amused by this story. At the same time, I found it fairly repulsive on several levels. We all chatted amiably for another 15 or 20 minutes until realizing simultaneously that it was time to go. Almost as one, we stepped out of the office into the long hallway and there, before my eyes, was the most beautifully rounded contours of femininity I had ever seen. She had her back to me and was bending over and straining to fix something. Her loose-fitting white pants clung firmly everywhere they needed to cling in order to reveal her alluring perfection. I was mesmerized....I kept walking.

I snapped back a bit from my reverie and saw my two companions, one on each side of me, fumbling in their pockets and staring straight ahead.

I said, "Hey boys, I saw her first."

They each peeled off to the sides, like jets in a Blue Angels performance. I just kept walking straight ahead and quietly stopped in front of her. She had no idea I was behind her.

I said, "Hi" as eloquently as I could.

She turned around, this radiant beauty with long auburn hair flowing to the middle of her back and gorgeous big blue eyes, and she said to me, "Well are you going to just stand there or are you going to help me?"

And that is how I met my beautiful Lisa, my Lara.

Well, next day I looked around the hospital and I found her. I asked her to come see my dog, Blacky. After work we walked over to my house that sat on the corner of the hospital grounds. Blacky had a large plastic cone around his neck to prevent him from getting at the wound on his left ear. He had gotten it in a dog fight. He was a tall, proud and very handsome tricolor black collie with a magnificent tuft of white hair on his chest. Granted he wasn't looking his best that day but apparently he did the trick. She liked him and that was a great start.

I said to Lisa, "Do you want to see my boat?"

She asked the reasonable question, "Where do you keep it?"

Pointing to my study room I said, "I keep it over here." and I proceeded to show her my two-man inflatable raft with plastic oars that I kept deflated under my desk. I had shown her my dinghy and she was amused. Romance was in the air, you could just feel it. Magic.

What began as a chance meeting soon blossomed into love. We did take out the rubber dinghy but failed in our attempt to row it to Fire Island. The big ships passing by and an attack by nesting seagulls on a small island in the channel forced us to realize that my pipe dream was a crazy and dangerous adventure. We didn't try that again.

It was a wonderful time. The rush of new passionate love is a force of nature, truly a blessing. It is the blooming, the flowering of the human heart. Swept by the currents of emotion and natural forces it quickly became clear that finally this was the woman I had been waiting for. It seemed ironic after years of fruitless searching how free and easy it was when I had finally found the right person.

Our lives had been a prelude for this totally unforeseen union. She felt it too. Beautiful.

Now it was time to head out, to leave my roots and find a dreamscape somewhere in the future that I could only sense. Horace Greeley had hit the nail on the head saying, "go West young man." It seemed that somewhere in the psyche, after years of American life, there was embedded a passion to go West, a place you hadn't seen yet but would have the power to make you stay and to unfold your destiny. Ah, to be 29 and starting out again. What a gift, what an accomplishment. And yet in some ways just the very beginning.

I asked Lisa to come away with me. It was a lot to ask. We had just met and she had had her own plans. In a shy way I proposed.... rather I proposed we go out West together and try things out. If it was a flop, she could fly back home.

She was game. We got into my little blue '77 Triumph TR7 convertible and split.

We travelled light. Blacky would have to stay with my folks in Florida. We had two back packs, a guitar and a tent strapped to the small chrome luggage rack that sat on the top of the trunk.

I had borrowed some money from Chase Bank since I was broke. Residency had given me an education but threw me into the world with empty pockets. Most of my colleagues had long ago secured positions in practices scattered in nearby states. Their futures and income streams seemed well laid out and all very reasonable. I, on the other hand, was of a mind to throw caution to the wind and pursue unseen dreams and hopes.

Now some would call this fool-hearted and risky but we didn't see it that way. I guess you could say simply we were up for the adventure. She brought along a few things including Doctor Bronner's miracle peppermint soap. You could wash and shower with it, use it as a mouth wash when brushing your teeth, you could even wash your clothes in it. What impressed me the most was the psychotic ramblings written on the blue label extolling its virtues and suggesting its many applications.

I knew Lisa was different than all the women I had ever met. She was a total anomaly for a girl from Long Island. Her family had a small house on six acres with a horse and goat, dogs and cats. There were chickens roosting in the trees. The family had every convenience but they enjoyed cooking and heating the house on a wood stove. This little haven tucked away in suburbia was a splendid island of individuality and pioneer spirit.

She was so witty and intuitive, so funny, intelligent and, as I was to discover, a nurturing daughter of Mother Nature. The miracle of two kindred spirits like us meeting by chance, two fish out of water in a polyester world, was amazing.

She was mysteriously modest. Most beautiful people are affected by the attention they draw. That is understandable. It's natural to feel a certain element of conceit. But Lisa was so different. She loved the afflicted, the poor, the stunted in life. She searched for a person's inner beauty and was shy about her own. Life rewarded her with a heart so big it could make you weep. She would not just give money to the lady with the kids and the sign at the Walmart exit. She would take that lady inside and buy her a basketful of groceries. She fed birds, loved nature and picked up trash on the beach until she got so sunburned she had to quit. She didn't take a compliment well but that didn't stop me from showering her with them every day. Every day until this day when I am 70. I have always felt so good telling Lisa how much I love her.

CHAPTER 3

Rubbing Shoulders,
Passing In The Night

I WANT TO PICK this tale back up at an even earlier time. The year
was 1971, it was June and I had just graduated from Bucknell University. Most of the students had left town by then and I was hanging around for my Army physical to take place at a nearby base. I
hadn't wanted to go home and do it there. I'm not sure why. Home
just didn't feel like it was the right place for that to happen.

Lewisburg Pennsylvania that day seemed deserted in the summer
heat. I was still staying in my apartment on Main Street, just a short
walk from Stiefel's old movie house, the Campus Theater. There was
a bar with a bowling alley across the street, all conveniently located.

My place had originally been an old A&P grocery store. That's
what my landlord told me. He was an elderly man and had lived
in town his whole life. The idea that anyone could squeeze a significant amount of merchandise into 800 square feet of space seemed
ridiculous to me. But who knows? It did have a bay window and

it was really more than I needed. The Bull, as we called him, had been the last tenant before me and he had left me a gift. It was a big burlap wall hanging with the word LOVE painted in large red curvaceous letters that were joined into one continuous line. It was very Beatlesque.

Next door and upstairs lived several other students, guys I had known all four years. They had been my fraternity brothers. Everyone was gone except for Les. I went up the old wooden stairway and knocked on his door.

"Hey, come on in, what's goin' on?"

He seemed glad to see me and I felt the same. His living room was very large and fairly dark with a ceiling that seemed a bit low. The dark wood paneling did nothing to brighten things up. Les sat down at a table. Above him was a very large, framed poster of a painting. It was titled in bold letters *DER TRINKER*, German for the drinker. It portrayed a nineteenth century-ish Bavarian type older mustachioed man in period dress who looked like he was about to face plant into his tall elaborately crafted beer stein.

The poor guy in the painting had a look of despair and the Rembrandt inspired darkness of the beer hall he was seated in mirrored the lighting in which Les and I were now chatting. I must admit it was a depressing piece of artwork, especially under the current circumstances. But the thought that philosophy majors had been the ones living in this apartment somehow put things in a brighter perspective. I saw the ironic humor in the dimness of the setting and the hopelessness portrayed in the poster. Lots of fun had been shared in these rooms. It reminded me of the times before this time, before this make or break time that we were now encountering.

"Town's so empty, it's weird. I'm looking for tumbleweed to blow down Main," I said, sitting down across the table. "What are your plans?"

"Well, I don't have anything solid but I'm planning to go out to Hollywood and try to make it as an actor. I'm changing my name to Leslie Moon."

"Wow, that is ambitious Les. That will take balls." I was impressed by the vigor and courage Les was showing. Some of our friends had definite plans, graduate school, jobs and the like. Then there were others, the loose ends, people like me for instance. I thought that going to Hollywood to try and be discovered was insane, but very cool, and I told him so.

I want to briefly interrupt my story at this point to describe the circumstances that were operational at the time. The Viet Nam War was raging. Student deferments for the draft expired on graduation. That year they had held a draft lottery for the first time in our memory. I heard the results as they were announced live at night. We were outside in a crowd next to the college radio station gathered on the lawn of one of the dorms. The station had put up speakers so we could hear it well out in the open.

Birthdates were drawn at random and assigned a number. Low numbers meant going first. My number was 7. Les had a high number. He could safely assume that he would never be called. So I was happy for him getting a green light to go for it. Not only was he free to go but he had an idea what "it" was.

You can't overestimate how precious and vital it is to have a defined goal.... just be very careful who you become in the process.

What are you up to?" Les asked.

"Well, I'm dealing with a low draft number and my physical is tomorrow"

"Holy shit, what are you going to do?"

"I have a condition that is grounds for a medical exclusion. I never appreciated having migraines until now. I think I'll be alright. After that though...I don't really know what I'll do. I gotta tell you, I'm feeling lost, I'm putting one foot in front of the other."

That was the last time I ever saw or spoke with Les, but I did get to read about him and I did see him on TV years later.

The next morning, I got on the bus that the Army had sent to Lewisburg to pick up the local candidates for their physicals. I found my friend Roger on board which was really nice at such a time. He also had a note from his doctor. We didn't discuss the details of our medical histories. There was no denying we were really nervous. The bus filled up. I think we were the only college students on that particular run. Everyone stayed quiet, it seemed as if every man was a stranger to the next.

I looked out the window most of the way. The trees and flowers were in summer bloom but that didn't cheer me much. We arrived at an Army facility and right away we were directed to enter a large building. There we joined other candidates from the surrounding areas. The physical exams began without much delay. We went through stations where doctors examined us in groups of ten or so. Various indignities you would reasonably expect to occur in private were performed in assembly line fashion. I was not so thin-skinned that this bothered me too much at the time.

Next we were led into a very large classroom area. There were more than a hundred of us there and each had to find a seat at long tables with folding metal chairs. In front of each seat was a long collection of questions with multiple choice answer squares to select. There was also a number two lead pencil.

"Attention," barked the uniformed sergeant at the front of the room.

"Listen up. This test is very important to you. It will determine what you do and where you will go in the Army. It is not an IQ test, it is an aptitude test. Do your very best. And you college boys, don't think you can flunk out by putting down the wrong answers or you'll wind up peeling potatoes."

I did put down all the wrong answers but as things turned out it wasn't necessary. My friend and I waited tensely outside the building until we were finally notified of our status. We both were found 4F on medical grounds, we were classified as medically unfit for duty.

We were safe. We could go home and proceed with our lives. We embraced each other and we both felt a great sense of relief.

Roger asked, "You want some of this?"

He held up a small piece of paper, "Blotter acid, want a hit for old time sake?"

Who was I to say no at such a moment?

"Let's go," I said.

By the time everyone was ready for the ride back to Lewisburg we were both tripping intensely. We hopped on the bus and grabbed the front seats behind the driver. I was in the aisle seat. The rest of the Lewisburg contingent loaded onboard behind us. The bus pulled out and I must say the world looked fresh out that bus window. Nothing had changed except my state of mind. I looked at my friend and we both smiled broadly.

Then I turned around.

What I saw was a bus full of sad pensive faces sitting behind us. Worry and grief seemed to permeate the air. No one was making eye contact. They were thinking about going to Viet Nam, of being torn from their lives and thrown into an inferno. Suddenly I felt deeply torn between joy and sorrow, between gratitude and yes, the shame of cowardice. Those are not easy words to admit, but those are important feelings to acknowledge. So it was in those days.

CHAPTER 4

Thank You Father

I WENT HOME.

The open door, the love, the pets, the food. It was still all there. Thank you Mom and Dad.

I was starting to grow my hair and beard. Since I had no immediate plans, I went to work with my father at his modest textile factory. It was down on Straight Street in Paterson, New Jersey. He was there for years and years. It was in a real tough neighborhood but he never seemed to take notice. Father was a proud and upright man, tall and strongly built, he had a keen and tempered mind.

Though a man of few words he was very wise. An amazingly hard worker, he never complained of the toll his physical labors demanded. He had risen from being born a first generation American, then an orphan during the Great Depression. He was raised in an orphanage in Pleasantville New York. That is where he met my mother, she an orphan too. He would pursue and later marry her as a young man.

He started out working, like so many at that time, in the garment district of New York sweeping floors, pushing carts of goods, carrying rolls of fabric on his shoulders. He scrimped and saved until he could buy one quilting machine of his own, working it from early morning until long into the evening. His little factory grew until he had fifteen machines with hired men operating them. He was able to move his family from a brick apartment complex of hundreds of identical units in East Paterson to a nice roomy house in the suburban haven of Pompton Plains. A town on the rural fringe of northern New Jersey.

Now I was home and a college graduate. Father had felt it was natural that I should be working, so he took me into the shop and I was transformed back into a factory hand. He had been bringing me there for years and though he never had actually said it, I knew he had harbored hopes of me joining him in the family business one day.

I remembered the days of childhood when I was too young to do any useful work. He would send me in the morning to the little restaurant next door where Louie would make us breakfast. Dad always had an egg sandwich on a hard poppy seed roll and I would get a delicious fresh turkey sandwich with gravy.

Louie was a Greek American, really quite handsome, with thick wavy black hair, a slight accent and a very pleasant demeanor. He came out of the same hardworking immigrant stock as my dad.

Of course, I appreciated all that Father had done for me. He had sent me to a fancy college, made a fine middle class life for the family. I had tried to get into medical school but I had failed. I tried to muster my will to help out, to earn my keep, and in a way I felt I needed to redeem myself. He could see I was miserable.

One day he asked me,

"Son, what's wrong with you?"

"I feel lost Dad, I don't know where I'm going or what I'm gonna do."

"What do you think you want to do?"

"I think I need to travel, get out of the scenes and places I've been. I feel empty, I need fresh air. So I've been planning to save the money I'm making here and go to Europe, just travel and sort things out. It's gonna take at least a year to save that kind of money."

Then a miracle happened.

He said, "Look, I'll give you the money to go do what you need to do now. Get it started. Get it done."

I was shocked and a wave of love and gratitude seized me. My eyes welled up and I hugged him. It wasn't necessary for him to make such a sacrifice, to show me that he still believed in my potential. But he did. For that I will always revere him. He had taught me over the years how to be a father, not with words, but by his example. To be a rock for my children and in doing so to show my children how to be a rock for theirs.

He had breathed new life into my worn and weary soul and for the first time in quite a long time I felt elated and eager to embrace my unknown future.

For your diligence, unflagging effort, your wisdom and your love, for the noble examples you set for our family despite great hardships, thank you my beloved Father and Mother.

CHAPTER 5

Europe '71

I WAS COMING DOWN the escalator at the Rome airport arriving from JFK. I could hear my own soundtrack playing in my head, Credence Clearwater Revival's *Born On The Bayou* with that great guitar intro pumping out....

> "When I was just a little boy,
> Standin' to my Daddy's knee,
> My Poppa said son,
> Don't let the man get ya
> Do what he done to me,
> Cause he'll get ya,
> Cause he'll get ya now"

I WAS HEADED TO pick up my only luggage, my faithful backpack. It had everything I would need to live on the road forever.... just adding a laundromat and some cash flow from home from time to time. I wouldn't need much dough. I would eat light and cheaply.

I would sleep wherever I found the right shelter at the right price. Wow was this exciting. Already I was refreshed. I felt like a bull ready to burst from the gate. My eyes were wide open. It was October and I had an open return date on my plane ticket back home to New York. I fetched my gear from the conveyor. My backpack was fairly heavy and included a sleeping bag at the top. I was able to carry it for miles at a time but it was an effort. The pack ran from my waist to the base of my neck. There was a belt at the bottom that distributed the weight of the load around my waist and that made a huge difference. I loaded the pack onto my back and headed out the airport to make my way to the city.

That first night I took the train to downtown Rome and found a nice but pricey room with a view of the busy street below. I noticed a street walker soliciting customers on the corner. She looked to be in her late thirties and still alluring enough to keep busy at her trade. I was tired from my flight over to Italy and I had no idea where I was going from here. I knew I couldn't afford the room I was in. As I contemplated my next move I felt a little deflated, similar to the feeling you might have after climbing a tall tree then looking at the ground and wondering how the hell am I gonna get down. To take my mind off such thoughts, I began to time the lady on the street to see how long it took her to turn her tricks. I finally fell into a deep sleep.

The next morning, I woke up on nice sheets on a nice comfortable bed and my mind was much clearer. Hell, I'm in Rome, check out the city and let your feet lead you where they will. I took a ride on the metro to the Colosseum exit and getting out of the subway station, Bam! Before my eyes stood the massive Colosseum just across the street.

There is something incongruous about the iconic structure. At once a symbol of fallen dominance and power it stands today stripped down to its scavenged remnants by centuries of pilfering. Yet it still rises like an imposing giant that has been beaten down but not bowed. It bursts suddenly into sight as you emerge from the subway exit and you view it from across the wide boulevard.

I went inside the ancient stadium and contemplated the history of the immense skeletal monument. A monument to savagery, to the thrill of watching and cheering on the death struggles of countless humans and animals. I was having trouble transcending the depravity of the culture that would crave such entertainment. It said so much about the Romans who built and filled these seats in the days of gore.

I left the arena and walked to the nearby Roman Forum with its relics of the ancient civilization's civic and religious center. I entered through the arch of Titus, a marble sculptural masterpiece with bas-relief panels of scenes that celebrate the looting and destruction of the great Temple of Jerusalem in 71 AD. You couldn't miss the giant menorah being carried away.

Passing through this glorification of plunder and murder did nothing to further improve my appetite for ancient Roman culture that day. I took in the rest of the Forum. I saw where Julius Caesar's body had been cremated by Mark Antony, the temples and civic buildings. I climbed up onto the Palatine hill where Emperors had lived and I surveyed the ruins of the Forum below. I looked out over modern Rome from that vantage point, saw the bustling traffic in the streets and decided then and there to head out of town. It just seemed too huge a city to take on at that time.

I gathered up my gear and caught a train for the southern Italian port city of Brindisi. It lay on the southeast coast of Italy, on the Adriatic Sea. It was the site of ancient Brundisium. This was the port from which Julius Caesar sailed to Greece during the civil war to eventually destroy the army of Pompey the Great in 48 BC.

I pulled into a hostel and parked my gear. It was already dark when I hit the streets to explore the town. I didn't like the vibe I was getting. There were no women to be seen anywhere and the men all seemed to give me hostile looks. It seemed I posed some sort of threat to their sense of propriety. I didn't look like I was from around there. My lengthening hair and growing beard, my faded blue jeans, peasant shirt and tan ankle length leather hiking boots must have looked subversive.

I got the feeling I was being seen as a threat to their sense of masculinity and to the virtue of their women. Most of them were young men dressed in tight shirts and pants with stylish leather shoes and well-groomed hair styles. I felt like I might have to become a matador in a local bull fight with some of these guys.

I cut my sightseeing to a minimum, grabbed a quick meal and retreated to my room. This did not seem like a good start. I just wasn't fitting in though I was just being myself, minding my own business, a friend to every man, but apparently the sight of me was not in high demand with these locals.

I was happy to blow that town. In the morning I boarded the car ferry to Patras Greece. It was a beautiful day with warm and clear blue October skies. It would be a day long trip making a stop at the Island of Corfu. The ferry was a large vessel with a restaurant and it carried cars, trucks and perhaps a hundred or more passengers.

I boarded, going up the ramp, handing a man my ticket and passing onto the main deck. There was a promenade around this deck with an enclosed area in the center that contained a restaurant, bar and tables. Those seats were filling up fast with patrons. Windows surrounded the enclosed area all around. A stairway led to a second deck where there were seating areas in the stern and at the bow with rest rooms and the control room in between the two. The cars were driven over a ramp down below deck to the garage area and then the ramp swung up to close as a huge steel hatch.

Settling in as we got underway, I started walking along the railing of the promenade on the main deck and watched Italy fade out of sight. The salt air was refreshing and so was the thought of reaching the land where Western civilization had first so brilliantly blossomed.

Though I had never been to Greece before, I had studied ancient Western history in college. In fact, I was a history major and always had a keen interest in the study of mankind's journey from its roots to the present. Greece was the touchstone and birthplace of so much of our foundation of knowledge, philosophy and art. It was also legendary for its welcoming people, delicious food and natural beauty. After my rocky start in Italy, I was filled with hope and anticipation. Years later I would return to Italy time and again and I would fall in love with that wonderful land and its people, but in October of '71, I was more than ready to move on.

There was an interesting assortment of passengers aboard. People of all ages and many different nationalities were circulating on the deck. I could hear snippets of languages from all over Europe being spoken as I walked along. I began hearing English for the first time since leaving the States and I must admit that made my heart swell. I began seeing and hearing young people who looked like me, talked like me, were dressed like me. Backpacks were being toted by others. Many were shaggier than me. After all, I was freshly on the road. I hadn't talked with many people about my trip prior to coming over and had no idea who I would meet on my journey.

For the first few days after arrival, I had avoided contact with North Americans thinking I would try and concentrate on meeting locals. That seemed to be the right formula to transcend cultural norms and the social tedium that I was trying to outrun. But I had made scant little contact with anyone since I arrived and the sound of my mother tongue was sweet music.

And then I saw her standing at the rail looking out to sea, her green backpack almost as big as mine was loaded onto her shoulders. She had long jet-black hair and was a remarkable beauty. She appeared relaxed and friendly. I stepped up beside her. In a tone so familiar you would think we were old friends, I said, "Hi." She casually turned her lovely face toward me smiling and said, "Isn't it a beautiful sight?"

Oh wow, she speaks English! I felt comfortable for the first time since I landed in Italy. Between the frenetic tour and retreat from Rome and the short but awkward stay in Brindisi I had until that moment had the strong drive to keep on moving. Somehow, I suddenly felt that I had caught up to the moment, I had arrived.

"What did you think of Brindisi?" I asked

"That place was pretty creepy. I went out to eat and there were all these guys prowling around. They would come up to me and start talking in Italian, a couple tried in English. I just ignored them and kept walking. On the way back somebody pinched my ass when I walked by. How did it go for you?" she asked smiling.

"Pretty much the same on the creepy part. Where are you from?" Judging from her accent I was expecting to hear that she came from a northeastern state, probably upstate New York.

"Ottawa" she smiled.

Now, I had never had a friendship with a Canadian before. But just this little bit of contact made me feel that she could easily have been from New Jersey and from my hometown. I do have to say, it felt electric. Her thick raven hair framed her beautiful large hazel eyes and fine symmetrical features. Her perfect white teeth were encompassed by sensuous lips in an alluring smile. Her skin was fair with delightful faint freckles on that lovely face.

"How about you?" she asked.

"I'm from northern New Jersey, about 30 miles from New York City. How long have you been on the road?" I asked.

About 6 weeks was the answer.

We chatted like old friends. Her name was Alison McMaster. She was of Scottish descent. She told me about her adventure. She was 20 and had been living in a loft in Montreal with a handsome and passionate French-Canadian artist. She loved him, but the intensity of the relationship had become stifling and his sexual demands were too intense. It was suffocating. She had fled, travelling to Europe alone to sort things out. She told me of her trip through France, Spain and Italy and that she had saved the best for last. Greece had always been her cherished destination.

She had met many English-speaking travelers from around the world: Americans, Canadians, British, Australians, Europeans you name it. Most were in their early twenties, most were well educated and middle class and all of them were on the road. It sounded as if long haired backpackers from all over the world were converging on Europe with the same intentions.

No one had told me about this before I had left America. I had jumped into this journey with little preparation or preconceptions. It could have turned out to be a very different story, but to my absolute delight now I was not alone. She told me that Greece was at the crossroads of a migration of hippies and searchers. People like me with fresh eyes and hopes were traveling east to immerse themselves in the cultural and spiritual waters of India.

Athens was the epicenter. There was a tide running through the city, those heading east and those returning. It was a route like some sort of ancient silk road that led through Turkey, Afghanistan and Pakistan finally ending in India. I realized I had joined a human current, a flood of spiritual and existential seekers.

I had read many of the works of Hermann Hesse, the great German author of *Steppenwolf* and *Siddhartha*. He had shone a bright light onto the power of integrating the traditions of the East and West as an adjunct to self-discovery and overcoming a sense of alienation. My generation had taken that concept to heart. Maybe it was the Beatles' experiences in India that inspired youth the most.

Legendary bus trips of hippies had already been making this journey for years. The phenomenon was in high gear long before I arrived but it was all news to me. The desire for self-realization, the value of discovering new spiritual and moral footing in a world that seemed stunted was central to the cultural rebellion at home. It seemed as if suddenly I would be on the front lines of that quest.

Alison was so smart, so damned beautiful. Her shapely body was not completely disguised by her Mexican cotton shirt, loose-fitting kaki cargo pants with all those front pockets and her short tan leather hiking boots. She looked fabulous and I knew right then I was headed to Athens too.

We talked all the way to Corfu and then to Patras. That city lay on the western coast of the large Greek peninsula, the Peloponnese. To the northeast lay the legendary narrow isthmus and city of Corinth and to the south the famous city of Sparta. We decided to leave the peninsula and catch a bus to Athens on the mainland, not stopping in between. She had three weeks left on her plane ticket and suddenly I felt again the restraints of time.

I told her about a hotel I had found out about in a guidebook. It was called the Carolina Hotel and was run by two Greek American brothers from the Carolinas who had returned to Athens. They bought the hotel and tried to make a go of it. The place got four stars for cheapness, fun and hipness by the young pilgrims who had passed through. It was located in the heart of Athens just steps away from the ancient quarter known as the Plaka. We pulled into the place at about sundown.

The hotel was a trip. Around the lobby were milling young travelers who looked and dressed like Alison and me. I immediately felt at home. This was not Brindisi, that was for sure. I checked us into a room. The Carolina brothers were both at the reception desk. They looked like twins, both fortyish, short and stocky with the same gray pallor, wide square faces and thinning hair. I had pictured them looking quite differently when I had read about them and their hotel in my guidebook. But now here we were together in the flesh. This was fun.

We found our modest but more than adequate room and fell exhausted into the bed. That night we both slept deeply and in peace. I did not try touch the lovely Alison. She was recovering from a demanding lover and I needed to sort out my own sexual frustrations. That aspect of my life was an important element in the internal upheaval I was experiencing. We both needed healing and redirection in that regard. I think we recognized that implicitly in each other and it created an immediate trust and a deep bond. We both awoke with smiles in the morning and an urge to hit the street and see the town.

CHAPTER 6

Acropolis

It was a day of joyous beauty, it felt great to be alive. A new entrancing female companion, no agendas, no past and here we were walking around Athens, both of us for the first time. We had headed just up the street to the Plaka, the old quarter of the city inhabited since ancient times. The Plaka ascends a fairly steep hill and at the top of the height stands the majestic Acropolis with its mighty walls and the remains of the temples above them.

We started our day at the base of the Plaka so that we were never climbing uphill as we weaved through the rows of little shops and display tables with all kinds of colorful wares. The warm Aegean air was lovely in October with brilliant blue skies and tufts of white clouds. The smells of souvlaki and gyros permeated the air with a mouthwatering pungency. There were shops selling leather goods and clothes. all kinds of trinkets, replicas of ancient pottery, jewelry, musical instruments, you name it. In every direction there was a riot of wares greeting the eye. A butcher's shop displayed half of a skinned lamb hanging in the window. After a few hours, the crowds and the hubbub started to wear a bit thin so we ducked into a narrow street climbing uphill a bit and leaving most people behind to do their shopping.

We had caught sight of a lovely little taverna several blocks up the hill. It was late afternoon and the evening meals, the music and dancing, were still hours away. We were happy to get the only outside table on the cobblestones. We sat down on the wooden chairs close to the cool gray stone taverna wall. The small table had a clean tablecloth with a white and blue checkered pattern. Above it was an arbor adorned with grapes and bright multicolored flowers.

Out came the proprietor in his white apron and served hummus and pita with a delicious Greek salad of feta cheese, tomato, cucumber, onion and olives. Sweet and delicious Greek coffee and baklava followed. Typically, the beverage was made in single serving batches from strong crushed beans in a small silver-colored spouted pot that was set to a boil on an electric burner. Extra sugar, no cream, was always added without having to make a request. It had a lovely black-brown color, was piping hot and gave off a wonderful aroma. The feature that was most unusual to me was the size of the coffee cup. It was the size of a teacup that you might see at a children's tea party, holding maybe four ounces. The flavor, aroma, color and serving size was remarkably similar wherever I travelled in Greece. We both laughed when I eagerly drained the tiny hot cup of brew and got a mouthful of grounds. It was a rookie mistake that I wouldn't make again.

It was good just to sit and relax, to really unwind and look at each other. I was transported and I could tell she was feeling the excitement too. The Plaka holds a special magic of which I have never tired and this first foray was especially intoxicating. After lunch

33

we walked up the honeycomb of narrow streets and walkways that wound past the shops, restaurants and old flower strewn homes of stone and wood....higher and higher we climbed until the street led to the foot of the Acropolis. It was nearly sundown.

Millions of people from every corner of the earth....bringing their millions of individual perspectives with them....these millions have walked up this ancient and beautiful route to see for the first time that which stood before us now.

I can't speak for others, or even for Alison, but I can tell you that I was filled with a sense of awe. I do believe I have never been the same since, and much to my benefit.

I want to describe the Acropolis to you now, but I have never said it better than after my return to Athens in 1995 when I was so much further down my path through life. This is how I saw it then:

AT THE AGE OF 45 I had returned to Greece for a land and sea tour with a group of physicians. I had not been back to this fabulous country since I was 21. Back then I had stayed for several months in Athens, living in hotels and basements of locals who rented out beds for the night in the ancient neighborhood of the Plaka.

Late into the night, the ancient Quarter was filled with light and the sounds of music. From the rooftop tavernas you could eat the delicious local fare with a splendid view of the hilltop temples above you, while the bouzouki music played on and on. Locals would get up and dance in their old ways, stooping and rising, tapping their shoes with their hands and springing up, holding handkerchiefs that united them in groups. Their intricate stepping and swaying had been choreographed over the centuries. Wine flowed and they would throw plates breaking them against the floors and walls with shouts of Opa! Tradition and joy mingled and I felt connected to the celebration.

Just above the Plaka is a dark, quiet and empty street that leads steeply to the ancient Acropolis. It is the towering home of Athena, the city's patron Olympian goddess. At the height of ancient Athens's glory, Athena was represented by a massive gold and ivory statue that stood within the sanctuary of the renowned Parthenon. This was the main temple and the focal point of religious worship.

Her statue was considered a masterpiece of the ancient world. Sadly, all traces of it had vanished in antiquity after it had been stolen and then somehow lost to history. Many years later the Venetians cannonaded the Parthenon where Turkish troops had stored ammunition. The resultant explosion left the temple in ruins and without a roof. Centuries of thieves carted off the adorning statuary of the Parthenon and defaced and plundered the glorious complex of the other statues, temples and buildings that had graced the mount.

But despite these depredations, the Athenian Acropolis still holds a profound fascination for us to this day. Though skeletal, its ruins maintain the magical combination of enchanting beauty and the emblematic expression of the human spirit yearning to offer its highest exaltation, inviting the invitation of their gods. The forms are of the classical Golden Age of Greece, the elegant marble changing color from white to gold with the phases of the sun. These proud relics still look out upon the ruins of the ancient Agora; the marketplace where Socrates, Plato, Aeschylus, Sophocles and so many other towering personalities once walked._

I had the good fortune back then to buy an old British Leyland camper van and I was able to sleep beneath the Acropolis walls in the parking lot of the shrine for several weeks. For that time, each night, my heart was the closest heart beating next to this great monument. This clearly was the achievement of a soaring. brilliant civilization and I can truly say that I tried to absorb its spirit with reverence and awe.

Now I was back in the Plaka, middle aged and with a tour group, watching an evening show of local performers who offered a variety of regional dances in their native costumes accompanied by lovely Greek folk music. We were in a large dark room within a building at the base of the Plaka and I felt somehow confined. I sat there for a while with the others but my mind drifted to the golden heights I had left so long ago.

As if transported in a trance, I walked out into the night and ascended the narrow streets until, in the bright moonlight, I stood alone before the walls of the Acropolis and imagined the presence of the goddess Athena. The night, the silence, the beauty surrounded me.

There amid the wreckage of centuries and despite the loss of long-ago stolen treasures I could sense the grandeur and the confidence of the great human spirits who had inhabited this city. The result was the poem that follows:

ACROPOLIS

On the moonlit walking way
To your breast Athena
Above the narrow Plaka streets
Still filled with their bright revelries
I paused in the sudden silence
Beneath your gleaming walls
And gazing upward felt the touch of awe

Athenian epiphany
Thought transfixed in stone
Eloquent in your silence
Exquisite in your form

Soaring place of consciousness
Your brilliant sacred marbled dreams
Once fleshed against this sky
As if the gods must surely see
And hostile arms could never reach
How sadly simple it was to breach
When the tides of conquest ran

How they tossed from hand to hand
The crowning jewels of man
Left the temples' bones to bleach
Like stranded whales in sand
Magnificent whales in sand

And yet
As I approached
My soul pressed against the night,
You sang of your ancient heart to me
In the pure tones of golden light

CHAPTER 7

The Crossroads

OUR STAY IN ATHENS was totally absorbing. Often during the day, Alison and I hung out at the American Express on a corner in the heart of the city. This was not your usual bohemian watering hole. No, this was an unbelievable bohemian watering hole. Sure, you could get your mail there if you had any coming. You could use your Traveler's Checks and conduct business etc. But it was the café, with its unobstructed view of the street and the crowd of foreigners that it drew, that's what brought us back again and again.

It was a sidewalk cafe with a cloth-topped roof. The tables were open to the street which fronted on the famous civic focal point, Syntagma Square. Directly across the open square and recessed further back on its expansive lawn stood the Hellenic Parliament at a distance of one city block from where we sat. It was clearly visible from our vantage point.

On the left side of the square stood the elegant Hotel Grand Bretagne where I would spend a few nights on my return trip in

1995. My tour group had departed and I had stayed on for two extra weeks.

I recall having a drink at the Grand Bretagne's bar one evening during that later visit. I was surprised to see a mass demonstration gather in the square outside the hotel. A large and angry crowd was chanting loud slogans about some economic issue. It might have been about how cab drivers were being treated, I don't recall precisely. There were signs being carried about. I couldn't translate the Greek epithets they conveyed but the emotions were clear enough as the square began to swirl with protestors.

I stepped outside to see what was happening. The crowd was in a surly mood and I sensed uncertainty and danger. I circulated through the gathering as more and more people packed the square. I couldn't really assess what was happening and I felt it inappropriate to ask the locals for details. I was caught up in a dramatic spectacle without knowing where events were headed. It was frightening and exhilarating simultaneously.

Gradually tempers simmered and the crowd slowly and quietly dispersed just about an hour and a half after the gathering had started. This was democracy in action. I was relieved that no rioting or police violence had broken out. Not on that night. But there had been numerous bloody political protests over the last century occurring in this storied square.

German, British and Greek tanks had rumbled through these streets in their turn. History had played out on this stage, with violence ebbing and flowing. In 1944 a crowd of some 200,000 tried to gather in this same square until the outbreak of shooting by Greek royalist troops left 29 dead and 149 wounded.

That clash had occurred after the Nazis had withdrawn from the country. Elements of the British Army intervened in the confrontation between opposing Greek guerrilla groups vying to fill the political vacuum the war had created. The British effort was intended to thwart the rising prominence of the Communist resistance forces, forces that had played a major role in the partisan struggle against the Nazis. Eventually, it required a vicious and prolonged civil war to resolve this power struggle. The shooting stopped officially in 1949, but the scars of that conflict have yet to fully heal.

Those were ghosts from the past. Walking around Syntagma Square in 1971 with Alison on a calm October day, you would not have suspected that such events had unfolded here. On such tranquil afternoons a stroll around the square was a relaxing pleasure. In front of the Parliament, you could watch the Evzones, traditionally clad soldiers strutting slowly with their rifles. They wore skirted tunics that came down to their mid thighs and a red beret with a tassel. Long stockings and a very interesting pair of shoes adorned with a red pompom on the tips of the toes completed the strange and distinctive ensemble.

Though they didn't look fierce, they were in fact crack infantry troops who guarded the Tomb of the Unknown Soldier. Before the Nazis intervened with their military machine in 1941, brave men such as these had repelled a numerically superior Italian invasion force, driving them through the mountains and back into Albania. Back past where they had started. The enemy called these Greeks "the wind" because they seemed to come out of nowhere and overwhelm them on all sides.

Everything seemed serene and in good order when viewed from the spot where Alison and I relaxed at the cafe. Behind the Parliament area was a park and a zoo, always a fun diversion. The streets around the square were continuously teeming with citizens going in all directions.

On the corner opposite the cafe was a stairway leading down to the underground subway. There you could catch a cheap ride to the port at Piraeus and easily find a ferry to take you to any island you might want to visit. On your way to the port, you would emerge above ground and pass the ancient Athenian marketplace, the Agora, just outside your left window. There was no extra charge for the view of the Agora.

Invariably, when we would sit at the American Express Cafe, we would meet young international travelers with interesting stories. Just as Alison had described it, Athens was the hub through which those heading eastward would cross paths with those who were returning and this cafe was the nexus of that activity. These gypsies traveled by all manners of conveyances; cars, trains, public buses, planes, some went in school buses painted in psychedelic colors. The overland trail led through Turkey, Afghanistan, Pakistan and finally India. Some even hitchhiked all the way there, though that took a lot of nerve. Many had been on the road for months or longer.

This cultural conduit had not been a secret and its presence was widely known internationally for years by then. Apparently this information had not been included as part of my college curriculum although that particular course would have been most helpful. With all the focus on the hippie movement you would think that I would have gotten wind of it.

There had been a Life Magazine article a few years prior in '68 about a hippie colony in southern Crete where a scruffy international gathering slept in abandoned ancient burial caves. Joni Mitchell had stayed there around '69 adding to the mystique. But I had never seen the article and only learned about it later.

As I had mentioned, the Beatles had brought Indian culture into the collective consciousness of my demographic and I had read many of Herman Hesse's books that integrated Western and Eastern values so beautifully. *Be Here Now* and *The Electric Kool-Aid Acid Test* rounded out my perspective in some respects, and I had an abiding love of history. With these tools in my arsenal, I was able to get up to speed quickly. I listened intently and asked a lot of questions. I learned each day and new ideas began to percolate as to where my journey might lead.

Alison had a return flight home already booked in a few weeks but I was free to go wherever my shoestring budget could take me. In retrospect it's amazing that I had found my way here. I had no clear expectations of the realities I would encounter when I left New York. I didn't really have a game plan. The sudden cultural disconnection after graduation had left me feeling isolated and more than a bit disoriented. This new atmosphere was beautiful medicine for my soul. I stopped worrying about what I would do for the rest of my life. I dove into the activity of every day with a passionate curiosity. *Carpe diem* summed it up and every day something interesting would happen.

It amazed me that I felt this rebirth of feeling and a new sensitivity to my surroundings. I had become so bored with the repetitive familiarity of my life at home that it had become oppressive in a way. Over the years since, I have come to realize how good a tonic immersion into a different culture can be, even for just a few weeks. It has never failed to energize and inspire me and I do it as often and for as long as I reasonably can.

There was something that struck me right away about most of the English-speaking travelers I met. It was an amazingly consistent thing. People seemed genuinely open and honest. You might have just met someone and within a few sentences a bond of familiarity and a vague sense of shared vulnerability would develop. People just seemed to open up with an intimate trust that would rarely have happened at home, even after a prolonged acquaintance. You just felt comfortable with each other, each slightly on the outside looking in, glad to be sharing an 'at home' moment so far away from home.

One lovely sunny morning Alison I were enjoying Greek coffee and pastries at our cafe haunt when we met a very colorfully dressed individual named Billy.

He introduced himself, "Hi, my name is Billy, Billy Bleach...like the product."

We asked him to join us at our table. He smiled, shook our hands and sat down. Well, how could you not like a guy like that? He was very friendly and had a great sense of humor. Billy also told a story really well and he had plenty of them to tell. In the coming weeks he and I would meet up again in Athens and then travel together for a month or so. That story can wait until later, but for now I want to tell you more about Mr. Bleach and give you a few examples of the road lore he related to us.

CHAPTER 8

Sgt Pepper

HE WAS A COLORFUL character, you'd have to say that. Though his name was Billy, I liked to call him Sgt Pepper and he enjoyed it when I did. It made him laugh. He was of average height, slim with long stringy light brown hair that hung down a bit below his shoulders.

What sealed the deal for the Sgt Pepper image was his ever-present coat. It was a long bright multicolored cloth affair that draped down almost to his knees. He always wore it unbuttoned. It had fur trim around the collar that extended to the hem, encircling the bottom of the garment. The cuffs were 4 inches wide with some nice, embroidered gold braid work. It gave him the appearance of a wizard without a hat and the image was accentuated by his scraggly mustache and beard. He had picked up the coat somewhere in Morocco and it was made of a fabric light enough to suit the Moroccan evening chill without overheating him during the hot African days. His blue jeans had lots of assorted colorful patches and his leather cowboy boots completed the wardrobe.

Bill was a cool cat. He told us how one fine day he was sitting in a cafe outside Casablanca. He was very, very stoned on hashish, relaxed and quietly watching the world turn. Beautiful thoughts and flushes of warmth made him slouch a bit in his chair as his mind drifted nicely. He closed his eyes and blew back a nice billowy cloud of silvery smoke. He rolled his neck and took in the gentle comfort of his shaded perch by the roadside.

When he looked up, he caught sight of two Moroccan kids stealing his motor bike. He tried to react but couldn't even stand up as the young bandits casually got on the bike, started the motor and drove away into the unknown. The hash had paralyzed him to the point that he could only sit there and watch helplessly. He never saw them or the bike again.

He didn't let that deter him any, he just picked it up from there and moved on.

Billy had a generous heart and he was a spiritual seeker to be sure, but he was also a hardy type with a tough hide. Originally from Texas, he had been working for a couple of years in the Saudi oil fields. He was able to amass what at the time seemed to me a small fortune. Especially when you considered my lean budget and austere lifestyle.

He had been able to buy a brand-new VW camper van. That, my friend, was the Holy Grail of travel lodging. It was fully equipped with all the accoutrements you would expect of a well-heeled professional type pretending to be roughing it; a working-class yuppie years before there was such a term. But this guy was a dedicated road warrior, committed to the journey. You had to respect all that. He had been very gainfully employed and that was really a sharp distinction from the other young folks I met on my journey. He was a couple of years older than me but he was a pilgrim like the rest of us. I loved the guy.

The Sgt would get to talking at night and sometimes tell tales from the road. He had been to Spain on the southern Mediterranean coast, the Costa del Sol. He pulled up to a small remote hamlet along the roadside in the late afternoon and parked the van. It was July of '71, late in the afternoon. He had picked up a couple of hitchhikers along the way. One was an Israeli soldier on furlough named Moishe and the other two were American guys, long haired backpackers with no particular destination in mind.

The tiny town was very unusual. The houses were all built into large masses of grass-covered earth so that the roofs looked like lawns and the doors, walls and windows seemed to be framing a burial site. Close to the road was a taverna that was obviously the cultural center and watering hole for the local population.

After they parked, Moishe and one of the other fellows, Willie from Buffalo, decided to hang out in the van. They were tired and were saving their money, planning to sleep in the van that night. Bill and the other American, Rick from Sparta, NJ, went into the tavern.

It was surprisingly comfortable inside. The bar counter itself was modest but nicely fashioned out of dark wood and it was well attended by local patrons. They seemed in good spirits and the drinking was getting started in earnest. The boys joined in and ordered the town wine, the *puebla*. It was a sweet red variety, delicious and, as it turned out, very potent. Calamari, octopus and *paella Valenciana* were ordered and consumed *con mucho gusto*. A guitar came out and a few men sang. Not a word of English was heard unless Billy or Rick spoke up. Life was feeling bright and beautiful. More wine followed.

Night fell and the Sgt took a good look around. The remoteness of the place and the simplicity of the people made him feel as if he had entered another world. There were few vestiges of modernity anywhere to be seen except for the color TV above the bar. That was the one modern anomaly that had struck Billy's eye when he first sat down but he had forgotten about it after the first bottle of wine.

Suddenly all eyes turned to the TV and the talking ceased. Everyone watched in various stages of amazement as the Saturn V rocket of Apollo 15 blasted off from Cape Kennedy on its way to land on the moon.

This was too much. The world had abruptly caught up with Billy. He was completely unaware of the space program's plan to launch. It seemed to trigger mildly bizarre feelings that were difficult to describe. The wine, the moon launch, his and Rick's incongruous presence in this remote place made the scene seem surreal. The room remained quiet for several minutes until after the rocket's fiery tail had disappeared into the Florida sky.

It was hard to know what their Spanish hosts were thinking about all of this. Whatever it was, they all seemed to react roughly in the same way. Bill thought he caught a passing hostile look from one of the men and then maybe another. He was becoming aware that he and Rick were looking like two long haired hippie aliens who had mysteriously landed, uninvited I might add, on the surface of their Spanish moon. He wasn't really sure though. The jury still seemed to be out as to whether their presence was considered a positive or a negative factor by the community at large.

For the moment, things seemed to be staying civil in the tavern and the conversation started buzzing again in the room. Using his functional grasp of the Spanish language, Bill was able to have a rudimentary conversation with the barkeep. The man said he was the owner and lived in the back apartment with his wife and family. He mentioned that there was a room with two beds for rent upstairs if Bill and Rick were so inclined. The thought of a real bed in a real room was inviting and they were very drunk by then. The right price closed the deal.

The carousing continued at the tables and the bar as the boys weaved their way up the stairs to their room.

It was a simple room with little decoration. There were two clean and comfortable beds. They stripped down and collapsed, passing out. An hour or two later, Billy woke up. He had to take a wicked piss. He was wearing only underpants and he thought about getting dressed and negotiating the stairs. But then he would have to walk through the crowd and reverse the process to get back. It seemed like a lot of effort just to take a whiz in a toilet.

He was still very buzzed from the *puebla*. He looked at the window and then opened it. It was pitch black outside except for a big bright yellow full moon and countless brilliant stars. It was enough light to see that there was a low flat corrugated metal roof outside the window at the same level as the floor of the room.

Bill thoughtlessly made a fateful choice and climbed out the window onto the metal roof to take one long wonderful piss. He was a bit clumsy and made some racket walking around out there. Halfway back through the window, a clamor erupted at the door. It swung open violently and the light from the hall filled the room. There stood the proprietor in his apron pointing a shotgun at Bill with a posse of maybe ten angry looking Spaniards clustered on the steps right behind him.

The man was yelling in Spanish, he was *really* pissed off. He grabbed Billy Boy by the arm and dragged him stumbling down the stairs, through the busy tavern and then forcefully threw him out the front door. The door slammed shut behind him and suddenly he was totally alone, standing outside in the night, wearing only his underpants.

Now you might think this would be a traumatic event, it would be for most, but he was still quite loaded and then again, he was Billy. There he stood in the dark of night illuminated by the golden moon and the bright shimmering stars, nearly naked, in complete silence.

It took a few minutes to get his bearings. He swayed slightly. Not another soul appeared. Golden light shone oddly from the buried houses of the hamlet like something out of a Tolkien saga.

"Holy shit, what the hell did you do?" I interjected

The Sgt cocked his head slightly and smiled.

"It was beautiful, man. I had to relax a minute, just stood there and took it all in, yeah it was a beautiful sight to behold."

That was Billy in a nutshell.

CHAPTER 9

Delphi

AFTER ABOUT TWO WEEKS in town, Alison and I decided to take a bus from Athens to Delphi. It was a truly spectacular experience and we were both entranced as we looked out the window. The winding road up Mount Parnassus, ascending from the shore of the Gulf of Corinth, has been elevating the spirits of pilgrims seeking divine guidance for millennia. It is a breathtaking and steep climb through a panorama of natural beauty. It imparts expectations of rising above the affairs one has left at the water's edge with the anticipation of entering a region of transcendent spirituality. This is hard to explain if you have not made the journey and I had not prepared myself for such feelings.

I had simply gotten onto a bus heading for a place I had read about in the past but I had no clear idea of what I was about to encounter. I was to feel stirrings on that journey that I savor to this day, though I barely understood them then. It is of Greece itself that I am speaking. But then again there was my lovely Canadian companion sitting happily next to me as well.

She seemed totally at ease and comfortable. That gave me a unique satisfaction. I imagined she was feeling much more secure with me at her side than she had been when traveling alone. It was so good for us to be together. The mixture of our emotions was intoxicating. There are times in life when one feels firmly rooted in the moment, when there are no thoughts beyond the immediate present. It is a glorious blooming of the life force, a bursting alertness to the unfolding of the heart.

It was with this building sense of anticipation that we entered the mountain valley that harbored the modern town of Delphi. We checked into the local youth hostel and stowed away our packs. It was evening by then and the ancient sites had already been closed to visitors. We strolled up the main street to check out the town.

There were a few foreign visitors walking about; some young, looking like us, others who were middle-aged. Most of those were well dressed Europeans. There was a road rally happening that day and a fascinating collection of vintage and modern cars were arrayed in the parking lot of the one luxurious hotel in town. Its big circular driveway led up to the porch of the well-appointed lobby with its fancy rooms and restaurants beyond, the accommodations of better-heeled patrons than us.

The town itself was small and quaint but it was not remarkable architecturally. It had been built in the modern Greek era and was occupied by about 2,000 permanent residents. The town lay just west of the famous archeological site. We walked down there to check it out but in the darkening night, little could be seen of the antiquities from where we stood at the locked entry gate.

So we walked back to town, grabbed a souvlaki, some French fries and a drink and we sat down to eat our meal at the street corner counter.

When we were done, we ducked down a small side street that descended a fairly steep hill. We soon ended up in front of a solitary taverna surrounded by tall young pines. Walking in, we were surprised to see that there were only local men sitting around. They ranged in age from about 18 to somewhere in their 60's.

In Athens we had been accustomed to seeing men and women at places like this having dinner, laughing and carousing. There might be dancing and singing, live music playing, dishes being smashed. As we entered this place it seemed to fall silent. All eyes seemed to focus on us at once.

There was not another woman in the place and I wondered if the presence of Alison was somehow an assault on their sense of propriety. The patrons sat in small groups at tables with hookah pipes spewing tobacco smoke. We sat down, relaxed and ordered some ouzo. Soon the casual conversations resumed.

There was a metal pole in the center of the room. From time to time some bouzouki music would fire up from a small record player loaded with a stack of 45 RPM records on the cylinder. Then a solitary dancer would stand up. Grabbing the pole with one hand, he would dip and swirl slowly, methodically interpreting the music. I was sure he was reenacting a story imbued with deep traditional roots, a dance that expressed sincere and passionate communal emotional memories. It moved the local onlookers, you could see it in their faces. I could feel it too.

I was fascinated by this display of traditional storytelling and it reminded me of a film I had seen of Hawaiian hula dancers on a torchlit beach in Maui. Different worlds, different stories to tell. That seemed to me a strange thought to be having at the foot of the Delphic Oracle and it brought a smile to my face.

We didn't stay too long. Though no one said anything to us, I thought I was picking up a vibe that we were out of place and that we were not really welcome. Perhaps it was our appearance, or maybe it was our foreign eyes intruding upon their intimate rituals that was disturbing to them. Maybe the lovely Alison, being a woman and a beautiful one at that, maybe she might have been the tipping point. Regardless, I thought it was about time to go. I don't think she was aware of anything amiss but she didn't object to us splitting.

It felt good to hit the night air and we headed back to the hostel, she staying in the ladies' section.

The next morning was bright and sunny and we were happy to hit the streets and explore this new world that lay before us. The walk to the ruins was surprisingly short compared to what I had remembered from last night. When we walked past the town and looked downhill at the Pleistos River Valley we saw this: the spectacular ruins of the circular Tholos, part of the sanctuary dedicated to Athena.

UP THE SLOPE STOOD the ruins of the ancient treasury buildings that held the precious votive offerings presented to Apollo by the individual Greek city states, each having their own dedicated repository. For it was the god Apollo who presided here, the god of clarity of thought and music, of poetry, dance, healing and prophecy.

Every four years there were athletic contests at the Delphic Games as well as music and art competitions all in honor of Apollo. The ruins of his temple complex still remain and within it lies the precinct of the ancient Delphic Oracle.

The most powerful personages from all over the ancient world made the pilgrimage here to submit questions of the most pressing national urgency. The queries were submitted to the priestess. It was said that she would inhale vapors emanating from a fault in the rocks that would intoxicate her. She would then vocalize in unrecognizable speech. Her utterances were translated by the priests of Apollo and conveyed to the supplicants. The results were thought to be advice or answers from the god himself. The information provided by the Oracle was often enigmatic when uttered but uncannily appropriate when the outcome of the issue became known.

On the outer temple vestibule, as it stood in antiquity, there were said to have been inscribed three aphorisms: "Know Thyself", "Nothing In Excess" and "Surety Brings Ruin". I reflected on that for quite a while as I sat on a low stone wall of the temple ruin contemplating my surroundings.

There were enough unearthed vestiges of ancient former glory that I could easily imagine being transported back to the days when the marble gleamed and the gold trophies shone. When proud, powerful and cultured people wearing bright and costly clothes walked reverently along these very paths. There is a very fine museum here. It houses many of the artifacts that survived the relentless theft of the shrine's treasures. Theft that took place over more than two millennia. For me, the star attraction of the museum was the famous life-sized bronze statue of the charioteer. It was as if you could look into his eyes and sense his composed confidence.

Outside the museum, I passed the omphalos, a large stone replica of the legendary navel of the world that had stood at this site. Ancient myth held that Delphi was the center of the world. I climbed further up the slope of the mountain and onto the floor of the massive marble theater where musical competitions were performed before thousands of spectators 2500 years ago. Beyond the theater at the top of the hill, stands the stadium where athletic competitions were held. I sat in the remnants of the stone grandstands once covered in marble. I tried to imagine the sporting spectacles that had been played out on this field over the many centuries.

I made my way back down to the floor of the theater where the ancient Greek chorus had danced. The natural amphitheater was largely reconstructed and it required little imagination to picture its marble seats filled with an attentive audience. The acoustics were superb. To this day you can hear a key drop on the dance floor from the furthest seats above.

All the other tourists were busy elsewhere occupied by the sights below.

It was very quiet as I stood on the floor of the theater all alone. In that instant I felt suddenly transformed. The magnificent silent setting, the warm sunlight upon my face. I looked upward and felt my spirit press against the cloudless sky, the province of God as the monotheists see it, that of the gods as the ancient Greeks had seen it.

I flung back my hands widely at my sides and with plaintive outstretched palms, I sincerely recited these few lines, my offering to the universe:

Speak to the Ages,
Seek the right light
Loosen your voice
From the cloak of your being
From the form that bears your name
Strain against the fetters
Of this blinding temporal frame

Bring forth your poems to us
Laden with images

Grasped by the talons of clarity
And fused with emotional force
Themes borne through hard visceral labor
And suckled by Beauty and Truth

THAT WAS MY OFFERING for the competition that year. There was silence from the audience, there was no audience, yet I was moved to tears.

CHAPTER 10

Poros

WHEN WE GOT BACK to Athens, we checked into the familiar comfort of the Hotel Carolina. We parked our gear and headed down to the bar. There was always an interesting crowd and the drinks were cheap enough. The bar room was a bit smokey and rather small. The dark wood paneling and dim lighting gave it a bit of a hideaway feeling. We opted not to sit at the bar and pulled up a small table under the slowly whirling blades of a fan. We started drinking retsina and ouzo. I never cared much for the pine flavored wine or the licorice tasting liquor, but I did give them both a good try that night.

"I can't believe we only have two days left before you go home." I said. "I've been trying not to think about it."

"Me too. But we still have two more days." She smiled sweetly.

"Let's go to Poros." I said.

"What's Poros about?"

"I got to chatting with a guy in Delphi while you were out shopping in town. He said he had taken a ferry there from Athens. It wasn't a long trip, a couple of hours sailing along the east coast of the Peloponnese. The island is right off the coastline so you can see the mainland across the water. It sounded beautiful and a nice quiet place to kick back."

"That does sound like a lovely idea."

The next day we were aboard the ferry heading south to the island of Poros. This section of the Aegean Sea is called the Saronic Gulf. It is dotted with small islands just off the coast. It makes a lovely day excursion from Athens and is a popular destination for people wanting to get away from the city for a weekend.

We arrived at the harbor at about two in the afternoon. It was a sun-drenched day and we checked into a sweet little waterfront hotel in town. Our room looked directly across the water of the narrow straight facing the quaint town of Galatas on the mainland. A colorful variety of small boats lay anchored or were plying the water with billowing sails and bells that rang gently from their masts. You could see and smell the lemon groves on the landward shore. The colors of Poros town and its environs were beautiful with its rows of low whitewashed houses and buildings adorned with brightly colored flowers, turquoise wooden window shutters and lovely orange tiled roofs.

We rented a small motor bike and rode around the island. The motion and the pleasant wind were a romantic tonic as Alison held on to me tightly and we prowled around the narrow roads on the scooter. We passed through a few rural neighborhoods and small towns. It felt like we were one body as she pressed tightly into my back. We found a beautiful beach called Love Bay and stretched out on the golden sand between the tree line and the gorgeous aquamarine water. I was happy to be exactly where I was at that moment. But I was all too aware that our time together was coming to an end.

We spent several delightful hours, talking and laughing, telling stories about our lives and simply enjoying each other's company. We nibbled on the snacks and drinks we had brought. It was too cold to swim despite the warmth of the November day.

As evening approached, we headed back to the area around our hotel and found an excellent restaurant with outdoor seating right on the waterfront. The dinner and wine were delicious, the company perfect. After dinner we found a bar with live music and danced and caroused with the locals and tourists until we grew tired.

It was just a short walk back to the hotel. We had a great view from the window of our room and the moonlight shone in soft tones on the water. We sat at a little table with two chairs enjoying the scene. Though we had grown very close in the three weeks since we had met and we had shared the same bed most nights, we had not been physically intimate.

"Why haven't you kissed me, don't you find me attractive?" she asked.

"Oh yes, I think you are so very beautiful. I've been aching to kiss you."

"What's wrong then?"

"I don't really understand it myself. I want to hold you and make love to you but I know that's not what you need. You need to heal, and so do I. Pierre was so controlling, so insensitive. I know you were fed up with satisfying him. What you really needed was space. You had to escape and catch your breath, and here you are, and I'm the lucky one who got the chance to share this time with you. This time to sort out your feelings. That feels right to me, it's a good thing. I need sorting out too."

It was a time in both our lives to purify the heart's impulses. It was an important part of the rebirth that we were both thirsting for. We looked deeply into each other's eyes. It felt very close.

"I'm feeling a strange shyness now and I can't really explain it. I just want to be here with you Alison, that's real progress for me."

"Thank you," she said and kissed me softly on the lips. She smiled with that beautiful smile.

That was the last night we spent together. She flew back to Canada late the next evening. Maybe if we had had a few more nights together things might have worked out differently. But that wasn't the last night I would think about her. It would not be the last night I fantasized about her lying in my bed, both of us free from our demons, unfettered, ready to release the passions we had aroused in each other. Four years later I would find her again, but that story is best left for another time.

CHAPTER 11

Crete

AFTER SAYING GOODBYE TO Ali, I went back to the Carolina Hotel and started hitting the ouzo pretty hard at the bar. I'll admit I was really blue. I had to struggle to keep that feeling from lingering too long or too deeply. My mind drifted. I thought of Joni Mitchell's song, *A Case Of You:*

"If you want me, I'll be in the bar
On the back of a cartoon coaster
In the blue TV screen light
I drew a map of Canada
Oh Canada
With your face sketched on it twice

Oh, you are in my blood like holy wine
You taste so bitter
And so sweet, oh
I could drink a case of you darling, and I would

Still be on my feet
Oh, I would still be on my feet."

THAT LYRIC WAS TOO close to the truth and it didn't help much. But in the end, I wisely chose to be thankful for the time we had had together and to not mourn the loss. It was time to move on. But she was not the kind of woman you could easily forget, not by a long shot.

The next morning, I walked over to the American Express and much to my pleasure there stood Mr. Bleach in his signature coat.

"Hey Billy, how you doin"?"

"Fine, where's Alison?"

"She flew back home last night."

"Bummer"

"Yeah, right"

"What's on your dance card cowboy?" he asked.

"I'm thinking about Crete," I replied. "How about you?"

"Well," said Bill, "I parked my van on a lot here in town. I've been to Mykonos and Santorini since I saw you. Rented a motor bike on Mykonos. Had a blast. You could hop on a 32-foot cabin cruiser in town. The tourists would load onboard in their swimsuits and sandals sitting wherever they could, on the seats, the bow, the deck, legs dangling every which way, and they would take you slowly across the bay to Paradise Beach."

"That place was a dream come true," said Billy, his eyes brightening. "There was a bar with a restaurant that had rock and roll playing loud from speakers in the trees, all of that right on the beach. The sand was golden and the water was still warm and crystal clear. You could see little fish swimming around. Bathing suits were optional and there were plenty of fine-looking ladies. The night life on the island was great with restaurants and bars along the water's edge next to old windmills. They called that strip Little Venice. Clubs were humming late into the night. Never made it to Crete though. Why are you thinking about going there?"

."I took a couple of courses in classical history in college," I said. "Rome never interested me much. There was too much dominance, too much decadence and violence. I was more taken with ancient Greece and their refined spirits. Their arts and science. They were the true source of Western culture."

"True, when I think of Rome I think mainly about roads and conquest. I think about Emperors and buildings," added Bill.

"This country's history is so fascinating." I continued. "Before the rise of the Classical Greeks, you know the ones who left those ruins on the Acropolis, there were the Mycenaeans, mainly on the Peloponnese. That's the time of the Trojan War.

"Anyway, even before the Mycenaeans there was a civilization centered in Crete called the Minoans. King Minos was the legendary ruler. You've heard the legend of the Minotaur, a half-man, half-bull that would devour young sacrificial victims in a dark labyrinth? Well, they found the ruins of a very large palace complex that they think was his. There is a theory that the place was wiped out by a tidal wave that was caused by the eruption of the volcano at Santorini."

"I went there. Santorini was absolutely beautiful," said Bill. "All that is left is a giant rim of the old volcano. The main town sits high above the docking area below where the shuttle boats tie up. The caldera of the volcano is completely under deep seawater and huge cruise ships anchor out there. They bring the tourists in by shuttles and then you have three choices as to how you're going to get to the town way up on the top of the cliff. You can walk, you can ride a donkey or you can take a lift. If you're going to do it once and you have the time, take the donkey."

I laughed a bit.

Bill continued, "The streets of the town up top were paved with cobblestone and lined with whitewashed stucco buildings. The colors of the shutters, the plants and flowers was really beautiful. Sitting outside at a cafe and watching the sun go down was a life highlight."

"I'll put that on my to do list," I smiled. "There's a lot of history on Crete...it's also the location where the novel *Zorba The Greek* was set and where Kazantzakis was born. That book struck a deep chord in me and I'm curious to see the island and get the feel of it personally."

"Would you like some company?" Bill asked a bit sheepishly

"Hell yes," was my answer.

CHAPTER 12

South Of The Cyclades

THE FERRY TO CRETE was a very large unadorned vessel crammed with travelers. Most appeared to be locals returning to the island. They seemed simpler in dress and manner than the citizens of Athens. There were many families, some with gaggles of children. Many carried baskets of food and fruit or other items they had gotten on their trip to the mainland. An occasional bouzouki was seen here and there. The whole atmosphere seemed quite relaxed and communal.

No one seemed to take notice of Bill and me. It was an overnight voyage and there was a large open area with bunkbeds to allow passengers to get some sleep. There were no partitions to separate the beds and give even the illusion of privacy. The other passengers seemed totally comfortable with this arrangement. Billy took the top and I crawled into the bottom bunk. There was homemade music in the air and lots of conversations swirling about in Greek.

The sleeping area had a view of the starry nighttime sky. The ambiance cast a soothing effect on us. Almost immediately the two of us were lulled into a deep sleep as the ship gently rocked and rode the

Aegean. Her waters had looked so beautiful at twilight, the "wine red sea" as Homer had described it.

When I awoke in the morning, after checking my possessions to make sure nothing had disappeared during the night, I went over to the port side rail to get a look. We were anchored in Heraklion harbor. The sky was a stunning azure blue with tufts of white clouds scattered about. The air was fresh and a hodgepodge of boats of various sizes floated around us, here a small fishing boat with nets on deck, there a long fancy yacht of some fortunate soul who appeared to be traveling in another dimension than the one I was experiencing.

I looked up into the sky and a large black flock of hundreds of small birds flew by in a mass and then suddenly turned in unison on the wing. The color and shape of the flock changed in an instant flashing as if it were a single mass. Smiling, I looked at the flock fluttering away and thought that this had to be a good omen. The salt air was heavily scented with pleasant fragrances from the harbor. The scene was alerting and refreshing. Anticipation began to well up inside me. Billy was stirring as the other passengers were already beginning to disembark. Soon we loaded our gear onto our backs and got on the line to go ashore. Slowly we filed forward until finally planting our feet onto the sunny soil of Crete.

"What do you say Billy, should we catch some breakfast?"

"Sounds right."

The harbor area itself wasn't much to look at but we were able to catch a good tasting cheap breakfast and get our bearings. We didn't really have a plan which was exhilarating in its own way. There was always the risk of missing something important through ignorance and lack of preparation but the unfolding of surprises in an exciting new place was an irresistible combination for the two of us. So we dove in headfirst. It was a short walk to the bus station and we headed immediately for the Palace of Minos at Knossos.

On the short ride over to the ruins we chatted about our impressions of Greece so far.

"You know Bill, I do believe this has opened me up in a way I never knew before. I'm starting to see life in layers."

"What do you mean?"

"Well, you've left the subway station in Athens at the Acropolis stop, right?

"More than a few times." he said.

"I've stood there in wonder staring at the Acropolis with all its treasures high above the exit. You can see it through the opening between two street corners as you enter Monastraki Square. Then you look around the square, over there is a Byzantine monastery and over there is an Ottoman Mosque. The streets are filled with shoppers and people hurrying around, just living their lives. Maybe they're going to work or whatever. Meanwhile they're walking by a trench where there are men working on an archeological dig. They don't even seem to notice."

I could see Bill's wheels starting to turn. He said, "You could see how they might have gotten used to it. Maybe it just feels like a walk through the neighborhood. That's some neighborhood."

"Exactly," I jumped back in, "but for me it was an eye opener. I began to see the layers of history simultaneously for the first time. It was as if I were stepping into a living archeology demonstration, a real-life diorama in a giant museum. That's what made it so amazing. I'm seeing it for the first time while the people around me are living their normal lives. Over here I see the ancient pagan monuments, over there a Roman monastery built during the thousand plus years of Christianity, on the next corner is a mosque that survives after 500 years of the Ottomans. One layer after another, all exposed at once. And through all those changes, the Greeks I'm seeing walking around have maintained their strong national identity. They're like a stew, a combination of all those forces. They are truly a remarkable people. A unique people."

Bill was seeing it too. He piped in, "They're very religious. You can hear them chanting on Sunday from speakers outside the churches as you walk by on the street, You can see it along the roads where they have these little shrines with icons and candles."

"It's interesting," I said. "I was talking with some Greeks about their modern customs. They tell me that many pagan traditions and holidays were Christianized in the early days of the church, traditions that remain distinctly Greek."

"You're really on to something," said Bill. "I could feel a draw since I came here but I couldn't put my finger on it either. At first, I thought it was the sights and sounds, the flavors, all the great people I met but it was more. It was something else about the place, something sacred."

"Right, I know just what you mean." I said, "Most people live on the surface. They deal with the present, not very concerned with the past. That's just history to them. Some people do think about the bigger picture, but not most people, at least not where we come from. Greece opened my eyes to the layers. I felt it in Rome, but I didn't understand what I was feeling until I got over here. I can see now how the past is inseparable from the present."

"It really changed you?" asked Bill

"It did. I've really fallen in love with Greece. The poet, Lord Byron felt it too. You know he died of a fever fighting the Ottoman Turks in the war of independence. He's a national hero over here. I saw the signature he carved into the temple at Cape Sounion just up the road from Athens."

Bill took this all in. Though he was by no means a scholar, he was an extremely intelligent fellow with a burning sense of curiosity. He was happy to be traveling with someone who could stimulate his mind.

He thought for a moment then said, "You're right. The layers are amazing and they're so easy to miss if you're just passing through. I think you have to open your mind as much as your eyes, otherwise it might all seem like you're sightseeing in a giant amusement park, interesting eye candy but just another notch on your passport."

"You mentioned the sense of the sacred, Billy. I can just imagine how the Holy Land must give a strong dose of that to the pilgrims. To journey to Jerusalem or Mecca and stand in the places where the events of your religion unfolded, now that's a transcendent experience that's easy to understand."

The bus pulled up to the parking lot at the Palace of Minos at Knossos.

"Time to roll," said Billy.

CHAPTER 13

The Glory And The Netherworld

THE RUINS OF THE Palace of Minos were fragmentary, but generations of dedicated archeologists had revealed enough of its gigantic floor plan that you could imagine a magnificent ancient complex thriving with life and humming with creative energy. The site occupied quite a few acres. It was not hard to picture the splendor and luxury that had once existed here.

Some reconstructed walls and beautifully painted stout Minoan columns, a bit rounded at the middle, were standing. Painted murals of thin, gayly dressed ladies with long brown curly tresses adorned the walls and gave a joyful and life affirming feeling. It reminded Billy of the wall paintings he had seen in the Minoan ruins at Akrotiri on Santorini. The obvious similarities of the cultures on both islands brought into focus a long-vanished sphere of regional harmony and prosperity. Giant amphoras and images of the sacred bull were in evidence and our very good guide took us around the huge complex indicating the presumed significance of various rooms.

She speculated that the stone chair we were seeing might be the actual throne of King Minos still situated in the remains of his throne room. There were murals on the walls that depicted men jumping over the horns of bulls. The guide speculated that the entrances to some underground passageways might be the source of the legendary labyrinth myth. Each year in those corridors, according to legend, young sacrificial human offerings were led to their deaths at the hands of the terrible Minotaur...

As the line of tourists filed through the remnants of this glorious past, we began chatting with a young Australian kid who was behind us in line, lugging his own backpack. His name was Jeremy. He had an impish quality and a great sense of self-deprecating humor. By the time the tour was over we had already bonded.

We got to the exit and all our heads were spinning a bit. It was a lot to take in so there wasn't much to say right away. We found our way to a bench and Jeremy joined us.

We began talking about our individual trips and quickly realized we were all on similar spiritual quests. It also became obvious that Billy and I had no idea where or what we were going to do next.

Jeremy brightened and said, "Hey, I'm going to another ruined palace. It's in a place called Phaistos. You can buy your tickets on the bus, there's one leaving in half an hour."

He smiled like a Cheshire cat.

Billy went for the bait, it just felt right.

"Let's go," he said, looking earnestly into my eyes.

"Sure," said I, and so we found our way out to the bus, loaded our gear and climbed aboard.

Now, before I proceed, I'd like to tell you some more about Jeremy. His was quite an unusual story.

CHAPTER 14

The Prodigal Son

HE WAS A JEWISH kid from Australia, a slender and handsome eighteen-year-old with straight black shoulder-length hair. Looking back on it now, he reminded me of a young Jackson Browne. His family had recently emigrated to Israel after his parents had had a midlife crisis and felt the need to return and live in the Holy Land. Jeremy's family had been well established in Australia for a few generations and they owned a prosperous business in Sydney.

The move came as quite a shock to young Jeremy and his siblings because the family had never been observant Jews. Jeremy had had a bar mitzvah, but like a lot of 13-year-old kids in the diaspora his knowledge of Hebrew never progressed beyond the requirements of the ceremony. He didn't understand the Torah section he had had to recite in the ancient tongue that day, but he could pronounce and sing the words properly because that is what he memorized at his lessons.

In reality, he couldn't even order a cup of coffee in Hebrew. So, his parents signed him up to attend an ulpan while the rest of the family stayed behind in Tel Aviv. An ulpan was a six-month Hebrew language immersion program and he was assigned to a kibbutz that lay just a few miles north of the Gaza Strip. The name of the kibbutz was Yad Mordechai and it was a very special place.

Like other kibbutzim it was a communal farm. It was founded in the 1930's by Polish Zionists. It took on the name Yad Mordechai in 1943 to honor the young militant leader who was killed while leading the Warsaw ghetto uprising. In 1948 the kibbutz became a fortified outpost when Israeli independence was declared by the UN. The full force of the Egyptian army descended on the settlement. It became a bulwark of defense in the effort to stop the Egyptians advancing from their bases in the desert and then rolling up the coastal population centers. The kibbutz valiantly resisted days of attack by some 10,000 infantry troops armed with aircraft, artillery and tanks. The few hundred defenders of the settlement took heavy casualties but were able to delay the Egyptian drive long enough to allow the Israelis the time they needed to consolidate a successful defense of their interior.

After the war, the kibbutz was reestablished. Museums commemorating both the resistance to the Nazis in Poland and the heroic defense against the Egyptians were created on the grounds of the settlement and have since become famous. It was into this mix that Jeremy arrived, ready to immerse himself in Hebrew and the culture of his new homeland. But it wasn't a good fit.

The first morning he was driven out to a radish field in the back of an open truck with benches for seats accompanied by other young members of the community. Each had been given a hoe and when they got to the site they all climbed out, formed a row and started clearing away weeds from the crop. Six hours in the hot sun punctuated by a short lunch break in the field were all that was necessary to convince Jeremy that this arrangement was not going to work out.

He pleaded with the ulpan director that evening to let him withdraw. True, he had signed up for a 6-month program but finally the director relented. He could see that Jeremy would be more trouble that he was worth. His passport was returned to him and the next morning he boarded a bus headed for Tel Aviv to rejoin his parents. He imagined a homecoming that was bound to be a most unhappy one.

The bus was packed with Arab passengers. In fact, Jeremy appeared to be the only Jew on the bus except for two young Israeli soldiers dressed in military uniforms who carried submachine guns on their laps. The young Australian took a while to settle down and relax. It was the first time he had been in such a situation since his arrival in the country and he wasn't at all prepared for it.

Everywhere else that he had been so far, Jewish Israelis far outnumbered their Arab neighbors but this border area near the Gaza Strip was another story. In truth the kibbutz now seemed like an outpost of settlers in an occupied hostile territory. He was very relieved that the soldiers happened to be riding along, it was a very vulnerable feeling at first and it introduced him to a sad reality he had not fully focused on yet. By the time he reached Tel Aviv most of the other passengers had already left the bus.

When he rejoined his family, the reception was as chilly as he had expected it to be. His parents were fully engaged in their zeal to be absorbed into the new homeland and this was definitely a setback for the family unit. Jeremy was the oldest sibling and his example would be important. However, after further reflection and heart to heart discussion, his parents reconsidered their sense of urgency. They agreed to allow him to travel a bit, to see the country on his own and find his own way forward into their new life.

So, he set off to take a look around.

He spent a few days in Tel Aviv hanging out at cafes on Dizengoff Street and checking out the night life after dark. Then he hit the road. He traveled by bus. First, he visited the lovely city of Haifa up in the north on the Mediterranean coast. Then he headed to Jerusalem. The old city was fascinating and he walked through the narrow streets with their stone walls and the many small open stalls of shops that were often just tables with goods stacked against the old walls.

It was getting on into mid-October and the chill of the evenings had already arrived in the higher elevations. He found a shop that was selling sheep skin coats and he bought one. The soft golden fleece was on the inside forming cuffs at the wrists. The brightly bleached white hide was on the outside. Stitched holes were cut into the garment to fasten the simple plastic buttons that closed up the front. It was nothing fancy but it would do the trick to beat the cold and the price was definitely right.

He headed out next for Ein Gedi, an ancient oasis mentioned in the bible as a place where David sought refuge from King Saul. It sits on the shore of the Dead Sea, deep within the Negev desert. There was a hostel there and he met several young international travelers who were passing through. It was an interesting place. The settlement formed a small area of greenery with lush palms and crops surrounding a stream of fresh water that cascaded down the hillside from a spring and thence into the barrenness of the Dead Sea, the lowest point on earth.

He stayed there for two days and enjoyed the guitar music and singing by the shore at night with his new companions as they sat around a campfire. There is something very special and intimate about singing like that together.

When you sing your soul feels free.

During the heat of the day, you could float on the water but you wouldn't sink. The salt content of the Dead Sea was so high that your body was too buoyant to submerge....

On the third morning he bid his new acquaintances adieu and boarded the bus heading south. He gave some thought to stopping at Masada, the towering rock fortress where Jewish rebels had committed mass suicide. They drew lots and then killed their men, women and children rather than surrender to the brutal Romans who were besieging them in 78 BC.

At the last moment, Jeremy changed his mind. He would return another day. Instead he decided to push on further south through the desert to the outpost town of Eilat.

Eilat was famous in Israel as the destination of the freest spirits and cultural rebels. It sat on the coast of the Red Sea with a beautiful and expansive beach. Jordan was visible just to the South. There were a few hotels along the beach but very few other buildings on the streets that stretched inland dissolving into the desert.

He soon found a comfortable place to base himself. It was a bar and restaurant near the water called the Red Sea Fish. International long hairs and rebellious Israelis had found the place years ago and it buzzed with young hipsters who were hanging out on the wooden porch with its big red ceiling fans. He checked into the nearby youth hostel and settled in. That night he decided to take a walk around the area.

The desert night sky was spectacular. It was pitch black once you walked away from the few town lights. He had never seen such prominent starlight. It spread out in a vast array from horizon to horizon. The stars seemed to have been just washed and hung out to dry producing a spectacular sparkling clarity and subtle variation of shifting colors. The moon was golden, full and huge.

Jeremy had seen a long gully during the day with some improvised dwellings built into the sandy side walls. This long wide trench was what the natives called a Wadi. These where dry channels cut into the floor of the desert. Their sizes varied but they were all formed over the millennia by the occasional sudden and teeming rainstorms that caused flash flooding. The one that lay before him tonight was perhaps 30 feet deep and 60 feet wide and probably extended for miles in length. He climbed down into the wadi and began to walk through it in the moonlight.

The scene was extraordinary. Beneath the brilliant shimmering black velvet sky, the walls of the wadi were punctuated by candlelight that escaped between the wooden slats of the shelters that the transient residents had constructed. It created a glittering golden alley in the night. Here and there quiet voices or gentle guitar music would emerge. Jeremy wondered, could there be Jews and Bedouins together inside? The peace and remoteness seemed a stark contrast to the political and ethnic tension that hovered, suppressed in the desert night, a danger reflected in the lights of the Jordanian shoreline easily visible as he emerged from the wadi and returned to the hostel.

In the morning Jeremy decided to head back home to Tel Aviv. His family was relatively affluent and Jerry had saved up some money of his own. He convinced his parents to allow him to travel to Europe. He had never been there as an adult, having been raised his entire life in distant Australia. He needed some more time to unwind before he would feel ready to return and find his own place in Israel.

He had mostly conversed with English speaking tourists on his recent journey and he had heard much talk about the road. Their values and tastes were aligned with his. Rock and Roll, surfing, long hair and blue jeans were his comfort zone. Peace and Love, that was the international mantra of the youth he related to. All over the world, young people were embracing the vision of an evolving culture in which old enmities might yield to a fresh blooming of brotherhood and nonviolence. Viet Nam had become the symbolic battleground not just of Communist expansion versus Western containment but the embodiment of senseless slaughter and heartless destruction by both sides.

Every form of Western art and media was screaming for an awakening of love and nurturing, of healing. But he knew that he would have to become more vigilant and focused. He would have to adapt to becoming a responsible Israeli. For in that land, violence was not a distant abstraction. The struggle between life and death still lurked around the corner of every moment waiting to strike and reignite the slaughter that the victory over Berlin had interrupted within living memory. Dreams were dreams but sad reality persisted.

That was the fate Jeremy knew he must ultimately face. He would not run away and pretend the hard choices did not exist. He knew he would have to don a uniform and take up a weapon someday but he was not ready to take it on, not yet.

His parent's hearts were filled with passion by their return to the land of their ancestral origins but they were still Australians and they understood the forces that were driving their young son. They knew there was a risk he might fly off and not come back, but they were wise enough to know that he would have to make that choice freely. So with much trepidation, he received his parents' blessing and he hit the road for Europe.

In the course of his wandering, he eventually made his way, by a very circuitous route, to the ruins of Minos' palace that day. He was happy to find us and we to find him. I was amused to see the little boom box he carried with him along with a nice assortment of cassettes crammed with my favorite rock and roll music. That was something I hadn't heard since I had left home. It was amazing how refreshing it was to hear it again as we waited for the bus to fire up and take us somewhere new.

CHAPTER 15

Pilgrim's Progress

THE BUS PULLED OUT of Knossos around 11 AM. We were about twenty passengers. The journey to Phaistos took a couple of hours. We passed through very varied and beautiful countryside. The curving mountain roads were heavily forested with views of distant snowcapped peaks in the center of the island. On either side of the mountains, the land tapered down to rolling green fields and orchards, slowly becoming more arid and increasingly barren as you approached the seashore from north or south.

Flocks of goats and sheep wandered about with their shepherds, sometimes blocking the road until they passed. Isolated homesteads would appear from time to time. We noticed that many houses were missing a door or a window. Later I was to learn that this was a deliberate strategy to avoid paying taxes. The property wasn't taxed until the project was completed, so the projects stayed uncompleted. We passed through a number of towns and villages until we finally pulled into the parking lot of the ruins of the Palace at Phaistos.

We gathered our gear and followed the other passengers out of the bus. It struck me as a strangely barren panorama. The ruins were arrayed on a small low hilltop but were much less intact than the reconstructions at Knossos. It gave the appearance of a bombed-out stone fortress where only traces of walkways and basements had survived. It badly needed a good guide to bring what looked like piles of rubble into proper focus, to bring the great value of this archeological treasure trove to light for us. But on this day, there were no guides, only twenty or so confused visitors poring over the stones beneath their feet, wondering what it was all about.

Looking around the surrounding countryside, there was no town or even scattered houses or buildings. It seemed a bit eerie. The three of us separated and wandered about, trying to make some sort of a connection with our surroundings but we all came to the same conclusion. We were not getting much out of this experience and it was time to move on.

It was then that we discovered we had lingered too long and the last bus back to Heraklion had left. There was still a Greek attendant there and we asked where we could find the closest town. I think he understood the question. He pointed toward the southeast and so we began our trek.

At first we started walking blindly through the fields that surrounded us in the direction that he had indicated. After about an hour, and without encountering another soul, we came to a low rocky outcropping and below us stretched a beautiful expanse of pristine sandy beach on the shore of the Libyan Sea. We had no idea where we were and the seashore gave us a much-appreciated frame of reference. Across that stretch of the Mediterranean lay Africa, that much we figured. Should we go to the left or the right. The man at Phaistos had pointed to the left, so we followed his advice and walked along the beach in that direction.

There was not a building or a person in sight, just a wide gorgeous strand of soft golden sand with low cliffs on the landward side. As we progressed, the shoreline intermittently turned inward giving the impression of a series of isolated coves as you turned the corner. Walking on the beach really lifted our spirits and I smiled as the Stones belted out *Give Me Shelter* on Jeremy's boom box. It all seemed so incongruous, so surreal, as if we had been caught up in a processional dance like something out of an Ingmar Bergman film.

After about an hour we rounded a curve of the shoreline and found ourselves on the sands of a beautiful semicircular cove. The sea was turquoise blue and gentle breakers rolled in under a late afternoon azure sky dotted with a few billowy white clouds and occasional darting sea birds...

At the center of the cove, and against the low cliff wall, was a small hand-built cabin of most simple construction. The door was open. I walked up and knocked on the door. A tall, handsome, well-built and darkly tanned man with a long, thick, blond ponytail answered with a smile. He wore shorts, sandals and no shirt.

"Hi," he said.

I was immediately impressed by his relaxed attitude. After all, we were three male strangers approaching his secluded digs unannounced. He was most cordial and invited us all in. I could see he sensed we gave off a peaceful and friendly vibe and that level of trust was very heartwarming in so isolated a place. His beautiful young lady companion seemed just as relaxed. Her long sandy blond curls cascaded down her back. She had warm blue eyes and a lovely smile. They had a few chairs, a bed, a table and a fireplace. On the wooden walls hung nets and spearfishing gear, a mask and fins. Fish and squid were drying on a line. He looked to be in his thirties and she in her late twenties.

We spent about a half an hour in pleasant conversation. His name was Jan. He was Dutch and had been an insurance salesman in Holland. He got fed up with the rat race and he and the lovely Liv had decided to make a stand here in Crete living on the beach by subsistence fishing and using their savings when money was needed. It was their second year of this idyllic lifestyle in the little cabin he had built himself. He had learned about the cycles of the sea, when and where to fish with line, spear and net, sometimes by moonlight and in different phases of the moon. Their supply of fresh fish, shellfish and squid had been more than adequate. They seemed to be very happy with their situation and they had no intention of returning home anytime soon. I think they both got a kick out of our little parade, our innocence and naivete. We were obviously lost and, in that sense, ignorant wanderers. I'm sure we must have seemed like a troupe of curious clowns. I know we were entertained.

We asked how far away we were from the nearest place one could get a meal and find a bed.

"There's a small town about an hour's walk further down the beach, you're going in the right direction," said Jan.

"We better get going then, the daylight is starting to fade." said Bill.

It would have been nice to spend more time with them. Usually I would have tried to get to know them better. They were free and independent spirits who had staked out a fearless experiment in unfettered living. There were no TV's, no radios or phones cluttering their lives. The simple joys of life were fulfilling enough to satisfy them. Their minds and bodies seemed healthy and refreshed. You had to admire their confidence and dedication to simplicity. I found them to be very inspiring, still do. We had our Walden Pond in America and these two had raised their own flag of Eden here on the beach in Crete.

We said our goodbyes and continued on our way up the beach. Rod Stewart was singing *Maggie Mae*. The Beatles, the Stones, Crosby, Stills, Nash and Young, James Taylor, Jefferson Airplane, The Doors, Dylan. Jeremy kept cuing up the tunes and it added a wonderful feeling of familiarity to such a faraway place.

We stayed pretty loose and trudged along eastward, but as the sun set and darkness approached, I began to feel somewhat uneasy. We were getting hungry and thirsty. Where was this town? We had no flashlights and things suddenly got worse when we reached a cliff face that terminated in the surf. That obstacle cut off any further progress along the shoreline. We would have to climb up about 60 feet if we were to continue walking eastward.

Up we climbed making our way in the deepening dark, struggling with the packs on our backs until finally we reached the top of the hill and found a narrow trail. We saw some light, then heard some voices and then... bingo. As we turned a corner we saw three young people clamoring up the path from the other side to greet us. Americans with candles, English spoken in the night, it was too good to be true. They were happy to see us. The feeling was most definitely mutual.

"Welcome to Matala," said Dan.

CHAPTER 16

Matala

"WELL AIN'T YOU A welcome sight," chirped back Billy, cocking his head slightly with an ironic nonchalance.

"Come on down the trail this way, watch your step in the dark." Danny called out as we followed him back down the rocky path.

I had never heard about Matala, though it had been famous for years as a gathering place of international free spirits and seekers of new ways. We had stumbled onto it blindly in the night but what a surprise it turned out to be!

The tiny town sat at the terminus of a valley that led to the sea. The single road into the town from the interior of the island ended abruptly before the wide stretch of sand that extended to the water's edge. A small collection of houses and a little taverna formed a row of buildings closest to the water with a second row quite a bit further back from the shoreline.

The small bay looked somewhat like a horseshoe if you were to see it from the air. On each side of the cove were gray-brown cliffs that extended to the water's edge creating a sixty-foot-high barrier east and west. On the side we had entered, there were Roman-era burial caves carved into the rock. These created clean empty chambers that the visitors were now using as their bedrooms. There were about thirty of these caves as I remember. Some were directly underneath another transforming one person's floor into another person's roof like a duplex apartment. No one had furniture, only what they could carry on their backs. Every few days the Greek police would come by and chase everyone out of the caves. When they left, we all would return to our own little shelter and settle in again.

Across the wide stretch of sand, maybe a half mile distant, lay the cliff on the opposite side of the bay. That cliff also had caves carved into it but these were much larger and were outfitted with the homes of Greek fisherman and their families. Their caves had proper wooden walls, doors and windows.

In this town the locals kept pretty much to themselves though the merchants were uniformly kind and helpful.

In the row of buildings back from the beach was a little grocery store. The old lady who ran the place was dressed in typical Cretan black attire and served delicious five drachma cucumber sandwiches on large home-baked fluffy baguettes she made in her wood-fired oven. We called her Mama. I ate plenty of those sandwiches and had a fresh Greek salad for lunch most days.

In the evening we went down to the little taverna in the middle of the stand of buildings along the beach. It was called the Mermaid Cafe'. There were a few tables and chairs that were always filled with fellow gypsies immersed in conversations as they drank beer, wine and ouzo. Laughter punctuated the air. The accommodations were simple, the chairs were made of light wooden frames with woven straw seats and backs. Blue and white checkered tablecloths covered the small wooden tables and the remains of fish dinners and Greek salads graced the scattered plates here and there. On one of the tables was a small record player with 45 rpm records loaded on the cylinder. All night long it pumped out the same scratchy rock and roll records that must have been played thousands of times. I never got tired of the sound.... and then it all struck me. This was the exact place and situation Joni Mitchell was singing about on her *Blue* album:

> "The wind is in from Africa
> Last night I couldn't sleep
> Oh, you know it sure is hard to leave here, Carey
> But it's really not my home....
>
> Come on down to the Mermaid Cafe'
> And I will buy you a bottle of wine
> And we'll laugh and toast to nothing and
> Smash our empty glasses down
> Let's have a round for these freaks and these soldiers
> A round for these friends of mine....
>
> Maybe I'll go to Amsterdam
> Or maybe I'll go to Rome...
>
> But let's not talk about fare-thee-wells now
> The night is a starry dome
> And they're playing that scratchy rock and roll
> Beneath the Matala moon"

JONI HAD NAILED IT. It was a moment I would never forget. I had put all the pieces together and realized just where I was. I smiled broadly back then, I'm smiling now.

CHAPTER 17

Welcome To The Funhouse

BILLY FOUND A VERY good-looking lady down by the beach to occupy his afternoons. Bill was a good-looking kid himself, well-built and handsome. Liz was from California and had been in Matala for a few weeks. She was happy to see a new face, someone that connected so well with her. The two of them disappeared for a few days. They hiked a little inland and found a large natural cave with stalagmites and stalactites as well as a huge contingent of bats. The two of them set up a little household with their sleeping bags in one corner to make a bed. It was intimate but creepy. The bats were no problem during the day when the little critters were asleep. Nighttime was a different story. When they lit a candle, the startled flying mammals would flutter about in a squealing, screeching flock. They proved harmless but it killed the romantic ambience and the love-birds were soon back sleeping in the burial caves by the beach with the rest of us.

At night we would often gather near the beach and light up a campfire. Everyone had their life story to tell. These were remarkably similar tales but still somehow each was totally unique. The common feature that connected us all was the drive to find meaning in our lives. We all had seemed in danger of hitting a dead end before we had hit the road. The forces that had united half a million young people at Woodstock, the dream of connectedness and hope, of new beginnings and the possibility of peace and love was the unspoken mantra.

By this time the veneer on such dreams had already been cracked. The concert at Altamont had happened with the murder that took place there at the hands of the Hell's Angels. Charlie Manson with his bewitched coven had already tormented Southern California with their performance pieces of terror. Viet Nam still raged on with full fury. In a way we were more refugees than pilgrims.

It made for a strange brew. We found ourselves floating in a bubble of beautiful possibilities. But it was an illusion, a Disneyland for privileged youth. The welcoming Greeks who lived in this town tolerated our hedonistic lifestyles with a respectful detachment. We obliged them with our discretion and it all seemed to work out. Blind eyes were turned in both directions.

Their lives were distinctly different from ours.

On the bus ride I had taken that day to Delphi, I had seen the date April 21,1967 several miles off in the distance high on a denuded hilltop. It was formed from what appeared to be huge boulders painted white. It meant nothing to me at the time but later I would learn it was the date that the Greek Junta had taken over the country in a military coup and set up the Regime of the Colonels. From that time forward fear and terror had gripped Greece. But you wouldn't have known it if you didn't dig under the surface and talk quietly to the Greeks you met along the way.

The people seemed generally relaxed and gracious, so natural in their embrace of life and its joys, generous with their good feelings. But the citizens had to be very careful as to what they said and to whom. People were being imprisoned, they disappeared, they were tortured by the thousands, some were murdered, sometimes because of simply having the wrong opinions. Everywhere there might be ears listening, ready to betray a dissenter.

Here in the birthplace of democracy, the wellspring of rational thought, here even music was being censored. I was to learn much more about this later, but as a foreign traveler stepping off the ferry in Patras that first day, I had been totally oblivious to these conditions. That strange and ugly monument on that distant hill was a mysterious first clue to my understanding of the realities of modern Greece.

Though I had studied classical history in college, I had not connected the dots all the way to the present. How could I have been so blind you might ask? It was all too easy to miss such fundamental details. This experience introduced me to the false sense of peaceful normality that deceives the mind of the uninformed foreigner passing through a totalitarian society.

The tourist attending the 1936 Berlin Olympics, the weekender in Franco's Spain in '71, the sojourner spending several days at Paradise Beach on Mykonos or enjoying the pleasures of Matala that year might return home with glowing stories to tell. It was an easy trap to fall into. It is the very illusion of calm and order that helps such repressive regimes to persist and to tighten their grip on power. On the way to Delphi that day with Alison by my side, such thoughts had not yet occurred to me. Sometimes ignorance truly is bliss.

This repressive government wanted to promote the economics of tourism. That is why they permitted libertine playgrounds to exist in their country as long as those visitors' public behavior was sufficiently discrete. In regard to its own people, the Junta promoted a rigid conformist morality of conservative values. Pornography was banned and modesty was insisted upon. It was not an environment that invited social experimentation of any kind.

Jeremy told a harrowing tale regarding this subject around the fire one night. He had met a Greek college student named George in Athens. He was a friendly and studious young man, well dressed with hair that was lengthening a bit, much to the distress of his conservative parents with whom he lived in the city. Jerry and George got to talking and George invited him to his home. They shared an interest in the same type of music and George showed Jeremy his prized possession, a red electric guitar that he could barely play. George invited him along on a visit to the island of Hydra that he had planned for the next day. Perfect, thought Jeremy.

It was a several hour ferry ride to the small, picturesque island in the Saronic Gulf. The harbor was crescent shaped with rows of well-maintained centuries-old stone homes lining the waterfront and rising upward on the sloping streets behind them. On one end of the harbor was a naval base. Everyone was expected to stand at attention when the national anthem would ring out at noon. The town was tidy and calm. It looked like a good place for an artist to hang out. Leonard Cohen had once owned a house here when he had lived on the island in the early 60's. It was a thriving international artist's colony in those days. That wasn't surprising, there was still a quiet peaceful atmosphere conducive to creative spirits.

Jeremy had been out and about during the day. There were no cars on the island but he had nearly been trampled by a runaway donkey on one of the narrow side streets just off the waterfront. He had had to jump to the side of the street and press his chest hard against the wall of a building to avoid being run over by the terrified, baying animal. That evening George and Jerry found a place to sleep on the floor of his friend's home. The other three houseguests were all Greeks in their twenties with long hair and beards, friendly enough guys though they spoke no English.

About four in the morning, the silent darkness was disturbed by the door flying open. Before Jeremy realized what was going on, the intruders were revealed to be policemen. Without much discussion, the officers roughly grabbed two of the guests and hustled them away under arrest. No one knew what they had been accused of or where they were being taken. Perhaps it was simply the way they looked and carried themselves. Maybe it was something they had said or written. George didn't know the two who had been taken away and had no idea what this raid was all about but it was clear it was time to blow town and in the morning they caught a ferry back to Athens.

This story was an unusual departure from the optimistic dreamscapes most of us were exploring. There was a real world out there with horror and pain reigning over too many destinies but we somehow had all seemed to have escaped life's gravity. We had come here to find renewal and in the process to rediscover ourselves. This was a time to revel in the possibilities of joy and sex. Oddly, while all this was going on, I was still in the monastic phase of my psychic restructuring.

A lovely little redheaded Canadian nurse noticed me and asked if I would like to enjoy her carnal comforts that night. I politely thanked her but explained that I was abstaining in an effort to get my head right regarding that very subject. This phase of reorientation would not last too much longer. Within a year I would be back in my testosterone-riven state of confusion, which I suppose is the normal condition of most young men.

Jeremy hooked up with a girl from Connecticut, they evidently had similar sensibilities and they were talking about finding a donkey and heading off into the hills. I knew this was a fantasy and I chuckled when I heard about this pipe dream. I knew he was processing his future and that the hope of finding God in the arid hills of Crete added a romantic twist to the uncertain destiny that lay before him.

We spent three wonderful weeks in Matala before we all split up. Jeremy was planning on going back to Israel with his Yankee girlfriend in tow. Billy was considering a trip to some ashram in India with a few of the folks we had met in Matala. He was planning to drive his van through Turkey, Afghanistan and then Pakistan to finally reach the spiritual awakening he sought.

Among the revolving cast of characters who were drawn to this place, I had met two Italian brothers and we had had many long discussions about the world, our hopes and our dreams. The international flavor was truly wonderful. But Joni Mitchell had gotten it right: "Oh, you know it sure is hard to leave here, but it's really not my home".

I said goodbye to my friends and I headed back to Athens. On the road you knew that the friendships you formed might not last. That was just a given and you had to accept it.

CHAPTER 18

Moving On

IT WAS A BIT sad to be traveling alone again, but you couldn't let that drag you down too much. I took the ferry back to Athens and got my feet back on the ground. For a few weeks I slept in the basement of a local Athenian in the Plaka for a few drachmas a night. I would sit on the cobblestone steps of the old neighborhood streets at night and watch the pedestrian traffic passing by. You could hear all kinds of music in the air. One night I heard Aqualung incongruously ringing out from one of the local clubs. Jethro Tull and me in Athens, now that was an interesting alignment of the universe, or so I thought at the time. It was very heartening on a lonely night.

I bought a rundown old blue British Leyland camper van, an Atlas Major, for $200. The steering wheel was on the right side as is appropriate for the UK, but the Greeks drive on the right side of the street as we do in the US. This put the steering wheel on the curbside of the road and made for some very interesting driving scenarios. At one point I drifted too far to the left and lost a side view mirror to a car passing in the oncoming lane. I decided to limit my city driving to a minimum since it was scary as hell in all that clamoring traffic. I drove up to the Acropolis parking lot and didn't move for another two weeks until the cops took notice and kicked me out.

I decided to head out of town.

I drove south and crossed the Isthmus of Corinth, passing over the deep channel of the modern canal. In ancient times, mariners would have to haul their boats overland to pass from the Ionian Sea to the Aegean. This led to tremendous wealth and power for the city of Corinth. Today, few vestiges of this glorious past remain other than the ruins of a medieval castle built on the old Corinthian acropolis.

After a quick tour of the castle I headed into the interior of the Peloponnese. I was very interested in seeing the remains of ancient Sparta. I had read the great Thucydides' historical masterpiece *The Peloponnesian War* written in the fifth century BC. He correctly predicted the spectacular legacy of his own city of Athens, it's physical, cultural and spiritual remnants. He said that Sparta would leave little structural presence for future generations to see, little physical evidence to help them judge the greatness of the Spartans at their zenith.

Thucydides was right. I camped out alone in my van at the site of the ruins of a classical Doric temple near Sparta. It was out in the countryside and overgrown by vegetation. It had been completely abandoned. In the day and night I spent there I saw not another soul.

Little more than a small rural town could be found when I searched the next day for Sparta itself. That was all that was left of the Laconian powerhouse. For me it was a sobering and solemn discovery. I mused, what might Las Vegas look like in 2500 years?

I headed back to Athens and hooked up with four Americans who wanted to drive up to Austria. At that time, Tito ruled communist Yugoslavia. Unlike the Soviet Bloc countries, Tito permitted travel by automobile through his nation. We made a few cursory plans and got ready to make the journey.

Before I leave Greece in this narrative I wanted to share a story with you that I was to learn about many years in the future. It says a great deal about this remarkable country.

CHAPTER 19

The Bishop And The
Mayor Of Zakynthos

I HAVE SPOKEN OF the Greek people I met on my travels. Nearly all were kind to me. They were welcoming and generous of spirit. I always felt safe in Greece, much safer than I did in America. I found this ironic since I had assumed the appearance of a vagabond. A well-educated, well-intentioned vagabond to be sure, but definitely a passer in the night. Certainly, the repressive Junta had made it clear to its citizens that tourists were expected to be treated well but there is something proud and noble in the Greek character and their hospitality that I sensed. Something that had carried forth from their ancient roots.

Almost fifty years later I was to learn of a most inspiring story. I stumbled upon it after casually following a series of browser entries on my computer. One topic led to another without any particular goal. Then by chance I read the story of the people of Zakynthos.

How was it possible that I had nearly reached the age of seventy and never heard about this before?

The year was 1943. The Ionian Greek Islands, lying between Greece and Italy, had been under Italian control since the defeat of Greece by the Axis forces in 1941. After the fall of Mussolini in the spring of 1943, the Germans took over command of these islands, including Zakynthos. It was well known throughout Greece how methodically cruel the Nazi rule had been in the areas under their control. How they had rounded up and deported the Jewish communities on other islands and on the mainland sending them north by rail.

Later they would learn that most were murdered at Auschwitz-Birkenau. They knew how the Nazis had shot without mercy many thousands of Greek Christian hostages as reprisals for resistance activities. Everyone understood the fate that would await those who sheltered the hunted.

I have read various accounts of what happened on Zakynthos but they are all generally consistent. The Nazi commandant summoned Mayor Loukas Karrer demanding that he supply the names of the 275 Jews who lived on the island. He was ordered to return with the list in 24 hours.

The Mayor was distraught. His mind raced in a confusion of anger, resistance and fear. He sought out the counsel of the wisest person he knew, the moral authority he needed to defy these bastards who would kill whomever they wanted for whatever reason they chose. So many lives were at stake now and they all depended on his actions. He went to the church to seek the advice of the Metropolitan Bishop Chrysostomos.

The Greek Orthodox Church had already stated its position on such matters. The Archbishop of Greece, Archbishop Demaskinos in Athens bravely issued an advisory about this in 1943, soon after the deportations of the Jews from Thessaloniki had begun.

He said, "I have taken up my cross. I spoke to the Lord and I have made up my mind to save as many Jewish souls as possible." He urged his congregants throughout Greece to join him in his efforts. Thousands of forged baptismal documents were produced and many Jews were hidden throughout the country as a result.

Now it fell to the Mayor and Metropolitan Bishop Chrysostomos to agonize over what to do on their own island. They were well aware of the torture and murder that awaited those who had the courage to defy the Nazis. These Jews were their fellow Greeks, they were citizens and neighbors, immigrants who had lived peacefully with the natives of the island since their expulsion from Spain in 1492 during the Inquisition.

The Bishop and the Mayor used the 24 hours they were given to warn the Jews and activate the clandestine network that had been prepared. They were able to secure enough hiding places to shelter them all with their Christian neighbors, mostly in mountain villages.

The next day the Bishop and the Mayor returned to Nazi head-quarters and met with the Commandant. He demanded the list of Jews.

The Bishop said, "These people are Greek citizens. They have lived in peace with us for many centuries. They are our neighbors and we will not let them be taken."

"Give me the list," the German abruptly demanded pounding his fist angrily on his desk. The Bishop handed him the list. It had two names on it, his and the Mayor's.

The Nazi's face went white, he stammered "What is this?"

The Bishop looked him squarely in the eyes. He was well aware that the Commandant might pull out his pistol and shoot them both then and there if it suited his purposes.

"If you deport our citizens you must also deport me. I will share their fate," said the Bishop calmly.

The German was stunned, never expecting such defiance.

"I have written a letter to Herr Hitler," said the Bishop, "it explains our position. Please send it to him."

"You have 24 hours to bring me those names!" bellowed the Nazi

The Bishop and Mayor left the headquarters unharmed and found shelter in their own hiding places. The letter and details of the meeting were forwarded to Berlin. Miraculously the order for the roundup was rescinded without explanation. This was a turbulent time for the Germans. The Italian surrender and all the setbacks on the Axis fighting fronts had created tremendous distractions. This relatively small matter on a remote island apparently got overlooked by the usually meticulous SS. Indeed, this proved to be a most rare deviation from their insane quest to kill every Jew they could get their hands on.

The Greek Orthodox villagers hid their Jewish neighbors until the island was liberated in 1944 by the Allies. The Bishop and the Mayor, all 275 of the Jews of Zakynthos and those Christian Greeks who had risked their lives to shelter them were finally able to emerge from hiding.

The people of this small island, which had suffered a long line of invaders over thousands of years, could once again freely fly their own Greek flag, these decent and heroic people.

There was general relief throughout the country mixed with a sense of shock at the level of destruction that the Greek nation had endured during the occupation. 350,000 Greeks had died from starvation and reprisals, as well as deportations to forced labor or death camps. This included approximately 70,000 Jews killed out of a prewar total of about 80,000.

After the war most Jewish survivors of Zakynthos emigrated to Israel or Athens. A devastating earthquake in 1953 destroyed much of the island including the old synagogue that had been erected in 1489.

Today at the site of the synagogue is a memorial honoring the Bishop and the Mayor, a monument to these two brave men and to the most noble and courageous impulses of humanity. But it was not just these two who were required to carry out this extraordinary act of defiance. Zakynthos had produced an intricate underground of brave islanders who risked their lives to save their neighbors. That required a cultural cohesion of the highest order and a community committed wholeheartedly to the declaration put out by the Archbishop of Athens.

This episode illuminates an aspect of the noble character, courage and spirit of the Greek people which has endured over the long and storied history of their vacillating fortunes.

CHAPTER 20

Epiphany

OUR LITTLE CONTINGENT PULLED out of Athens and began the long drive to Austria. Once we hit the Yugoslavian border, we took turns driving day and night, stopping only for toilet breaks and gas. None of us felt too confident about getting out and touring the country, though there were many beautiful bucolic scenes along the way. We finally crossed the Austrian border at night and parked on the outskirts of a little town. We pulled out our sleeping bags and fell into a deep slumber on the floor of the van.

When we awoke, the cold February morning air formed a steamy vapor with our breathing. I opened the back door to get out and stretch my legs. I had to push a bit to get the door to open. A layer of snow and ice had formed during the night. There was snow on the ground as well and a delightful sight greeted my eyes as I saw the quaint town in the daylight. Its scattered, well-constructed brown wooden chalets with their window flower boxes and shutters gave it an alpine charm. The town church stood proudly with its copper onion-shaped steeple dome typical of Eastern Austria. It reminded me of Christmas. It was definitely the opening of a new chapter.

While four more months and travel through many more countries would have to unfold before my return home, by the time I left Greece I had formed the nucleus of experience that would propel me through the coming challenges of life.

I had decided before I left the States that I would forget about long term plans and simply live for the moment. It was a gamble. I could have returned no further along than when I left. Indeed, my life's structure could have unraveled into further chaos. But that was not to be.

I gradually began to realize that a career in medicine would integrate my nature and capabilities for all the right reasons. I had a compelling need to connect with people. All my life, until I graduated from college, I had been immersed in peer groups based on similar age and social circumstances. Leaving this enveloping company after graduating college placed me in a void I had not encountered before. Suddenly it had become more difficult to meet and interact with strangers. I found myself feeling as if I were on the outside looking in.

The openness and easy intimacy I encountered on the road in Europe was a profound lesson and a saving grace. I had learned firsthand that it was the context of meeting strangers that made all the difference and that the right circumstances fostered the quick establishment of meaningful and intimate bonds. The practice of medicine does provide a proper stage upon which to gain access to our fellow human being's hearts and minds, to help them find relief from their physical and emotional burdens. I was sure I was worthy of that sacred trust.

The fight against disease, decay and suffering was a noble struggle against a definable foe. It was a good and worthy fight. I knew I would not want to become a professor of history or some other purveyor of theories. I needed to get grounded in the real world of flesh and blood for I was at risk of getting lost in a world of ideas. A world where I feared I would ultimately find myself feeling bereft of value and relevance in the end, left holding "an empire of sand" as the song lyric goes. I also knew I would need an intellectual challenge in my career. Happily, I would later learn how much I loved the academic aspects of a medical career.

It took a long while. The elements of this clarity had to marinate thoroughly and consolidate into an integrated insight. I never tried to force the decision. I had been given the luxury of time. It all came together rather unexpectedly in a moment of ironic anticlimax.

One day, I was sitting on the steps of a staircase in a dumpy hotel in Valencia, Spain waiting to catch a ferry to Mallorca. It was there that I had an epiphany. Unsummoned, the pieces all fell into place and suddenly I knew clearly what I wanted to do with the rest of my life. Why it came into focus at that particular moment is a very good question for which I still have no answer.

I was surprised but greatly relieved at how decisive I felt. It was as if my subconscious had fashioned all the psychic fragments together and then, like Botticelli's birth of Venus, a clear vision had sprung into view fully formed. From that moment on, I proceeded with an uninterrupted ambition to get into medical school and strive to be the best physician I was capable of becoming.

I was ready to go home.

CHAPTER 21

Bienvenido A Guadalajara

THE FLIGHT BACK TO New York was long but painless. I was buoyed by the energy of my spiritual reawakening and having at last found the right path forward. My game plan was quite vague but that did not blunt my enthusiasm. I was thinking that I would get a job doing something or other while I saved up my money, retook the MCAT exam and reapplied to medical school.

I must have looked quite bedraggled, rode hard and put away wet as they say, but I was completely unselfconscious. I had a year's growth of hair, mustache and beard. I hadn't bought new clothes in quite a while. This had been my everyday attire and it had not seemed to be attracting much attention on my recent travels, so I felt relaxed about my condition such that it was.

When I knocked at my front door, my mother answered and didn't recognize me at first but my dog Blacky did and he welcomed me with insane affection. You have to love dogs.

After Mom got over the shock, she gave me a hug and a kiss of relief. I knew she had worried about my safety every day. She was a wonderful mother.

Her eyes glistened and she said, "I'm so glad your home Son, let me take a good look at you. You need some cleaning up. Are you hungry?"

"Of course, what you got?"

It felt so good to be home with my family and for a few days I just slept, ate and talked. The first time I got to talk with my father alone, we sat together on the couch in the living room. He looked at me with a serious expression and said, "Son, have you thought about selling insurance?"

I chuckled a bit, I could sense he was worried that I was still as unfocused as when I had left last October.

I smiled, "No Dad, it's better than that, I'm gonna go to medical school."

He didn't skip a beat.

"How you gonna do that?" he asked

I slowed down a bit.

"I was thinking about retaking the MCAT exam and reapplying to an American school. That would take at least a year. Mom ran into my high school friend Spencer's mom. She said he is studying medicine down in Guadalajara, Mexico. She says there are maybe a few thousand Americans studying there. If you stick it out and study hard you can get licensed in the US or even transfer back and graduate here from an American med school. I'm gonna max out on loans and hopefully I can cover most of the cost myself."

He was very relieved and I knew he would help underwrite the project if necessary. What an amazing man. He struggled without complaint for his family and there was often little left over. I had borrowed as much as I could in student loans already but he had supported me through college making up the shortfall. He had financed my European reconstruction and still had enough faith in me to reach into his pocket yet again while I embarked on another four years of study without a salary.

This is a beautiful part of my story. Without the support of those who loved me it is hard to know how my life would have played out. It would be my honor to send my parents money from my very first paycheck as a resident physician and in the years thereafter to see to their security for the rest of their lives. That is one of my most cherished accomplishments and it was a joy to provide.

In retrospect, the hardest decision had been reached. The solid commitment to my career path had made all the difference. Now it was a matter of keeping one foot in front the other. As they say, the journey of a thousand miles begins with a single step. I applied to the *Universidad Autonoma de Guadalajara* School of Medicine, took a Berlitz Spanish course, got my hair and beard trimmed considerably and within 8 weeks of returning home I was headed down to Mexico for an admission interview.

Flying into Guadalajara was always interesting. It sits on a high temperate plateau with almost perfect weather except when it rains during the hot summers. The verdant palm studded hills around the airport made landing a lovely sight and this first trip down there felt like an extension of my road trip through Europe. I had struck up a conversation with a guy on the plane from New York who was a second-year student. He filled me in on the situation I was about to enter.

"You're going to have to shave off your beard and cut your hair way back," he said.

"I just cut it," said I.

"You're not even close," he said. "They won't even let you on campus looking like that."

"What kind of place is it?" I asked.

"It's a private university and they are far right-wing conservative. They are political rivals with the left leaning State University in the city. The UAG as we call the med school is anticommunist, anti-hippie, anti-drugs, anti-everything you enjoyed as a student in college. There are armed guards with submachine guns on campus and they're ready for any political trouble with their local rivals."

"Wow that sounds oppressive," I said, wondering what I was about to get involved in. "Has anything bad happened while you were here?"

"No, we just mind our own business and keep a low profile. So far, so good."

Well that was my introduction to the reality into which I was about to descend. After deplaning, I took a cab downtown and checked into a hotel. My interview was tomorrow. I hit the street and around the corner was a long strip of open shops under a single roof. One stall was a barber shop with two chairs and I settled down in one of them. The barber came over and put a towel around my neck, covering my chest.

He was a man I judged to be in his 50's with bad teeth and one eye that deviated to the right. The other eye had a dense white fibrous opacity over the whole cornea. He smiled and asked what I wanted. It was too late to run away.

"Universidad Autonoma," I said. He nodded his head knowingly as if to say "*Si, yo lo comprendo*" and proceeded to give me a buzz cut.

The next day, believing I was now ready, and very glad I had gotten the grooming advice in advance, I took a cab to the main campus. True to the New Yorker's description, I did have to pass through a gate with armed guards in military looking dress toting submachine guns.

They nodded to me, I looked the part of a Norte Americano dressed in a jacket and tie and sporting a crew cut. No show of ID was necessary. They pointed me to a line outside the administration building and I took my place with about fifty other Americans, mostly men, who all looked a lot like me. So much for the hope of a dignified personal process. I felt more like I was waiting on a chow line than seeking entry into the hallowed halls of a medical university.

After about an hour, the slow-moving line entered an office. I felt like an item on a conveyor belt that was about to be checked out by inspector #12. Finally, it was my turn to approach her desk for the interview. She was a young Hispanic lady, attractive, about 19 or 20 years old. She looked a bit fatigued but considering how far down the line I was, she was holding up damn well. She was friendly and spoke perfect English which was a relief given my spotty grasp of conversational Spanish.

"Welcome," she said. "I see from your transcript that you graduated from Bucknell University"

"Yes, I did." said I, trying to appear as bland and innocuous as possible.

"What did you do there?"

"I mostly studied"

"Did you go to any street demonstrations?"

"No...no never"

"Did you get involved in politics?"

"Not at all"

"What did you do besides school?"

"Mostly just my studies and an occasional movie. That's about it."

"Welcome to the *Universidad Automona de Guadalajara.*"

"Why thank you.... thank you very, very much," I said with a broad grateful smile.

I had been pretty nervous, not knowing what to expect. What questions would I be asked? Would I get in? Shit, between my haircut and my suit I could have been brought in on a stretcher lying in a coma with a check pinned to my chest and I would have passed that interview. Oh well, I was in medical school now and that's what counted. It was time to get oriented and to get going.

CHAPTER 22

Chrysalis Days

I WANT TO SAY at this juncture how grateful I am to the Mexican nation that took me in and gave me a chance to study medicine. A chance my own country had made too difficult to access for thousands of qualified Americans who, despite the obstacles, would one day succeed at obtaining the proper training and join their colleagues in the medical care of their nation.

The Mexican people were welcoming and helpful, the climate was great and so was the food. The immersion into Latin America was certainly different than my European experience had been but for me it was just another day on the road. This was an important advantage, for as I was to learn, most American medical students were far from happy to be in this new and strange environment. In fact, most seemed disoriented and homesick. They had chosen a path forward that committed them to leave the normal patterns of their lives and adjust to unsettling and unfamiliar circumstances. They dove blindly into an unfamiliar culture and they were treading water.

Once again, the phenomenon of expatriate bonding in a foreign place, that magic opening of the heart, allowed intense and immediate intimacy to occur between strangers. I found new friends everywhere I looked and that was most heartening to me.

I decided to work as hard at my studies as I could, to develop "ass power" as the physician father of one of my friends had advised. But I remained loose enough to still enjoy the immediate experiences of my life and not just endure the time until I could escape back home like so many of my colleagues were doing. I had fully awakened to the understanding that it is the journey not the achievement of goals that is the true source of satisfaction in life, that it is the process itself that demands appreciation and attention if one is not to miss the sweetest things.

The first order of business was to find a place to live. I saw a sign looking for a roommate to join three other guys from New York living in a house just down the block from the medical campus. Perfect. I took a walk over there and it was a great fit. I rented a room in the house and suddenly I was back in college, so to speak.

As I said, Guadalajara is a beautiful place with a superb climate, great food, nice people all around. It was a pleasant place to relax and get started with my newfound ambition. As usual, when in a new situation it was important to get your bearings, to learn the ropes. I was grateful for my experiences at the American Express on Syntagma Square and the adaptive skills it had taught me.

I asked around, talked to the old-timers, you know, the guys that had been there a semester or two. The focus was universal: Try to transfer back to a US med school. And if I don't succeed in transferring, then finish your degree in Mexico and go back to the States to earn a medical license through a Fifth Pathway program. Either way, there was a path to success if you doggedly stuck it out.

But how to transfer back?

This was the recipe: you study like a madman, you read the right books and read them in English, you prepare like an athlete for the Med Boards (more specifically the National Board of Medical Examiners Part I). This exam covered the basic sciences taught in the first two years at US medical schools.

Every medical student in America had to take this test and it was also available to those studying in foreign schools as well. Not only could a great performance buy you a ticket to an MD from a school at home, but it was also a chance to see how your test results compared to the students taught at the vaunted American schools (the relatively spoon-fed as they seemed to me).

This latter point was important to those who had been rejected on their first round of applications. They believed they were just as capable as those who had been admitted. There was plenty to prove to yourself and the challenge was invigorating. No one ever talked about it but we were all somewhat wounded by the initial rejection.

So you made the pilgrimage to Sandy's Book Store in the Chapelita section of town. You talked with your fellow students and found out what books were the best to read in order to achieve academic mastery of each subject. Occasionally there would be two recommendations so you would read and memorize both. Anatomy atlases and biochemistry charts were pictorial methods of learning. You got the feeling that you were being given a map to follow and that having a sense of direction would prove invaluable. In retrospect the advice I received was spot on and indeed if you mastered these academic materials you would be able to master the National Boards, that Mount Everest of challenges. And so the training began for the mental Olympics that lay ahead. It was humbling if you thought about it. I didn't think about it. I relaxed and took it one step at a time.

I bought the makings of a desk using cinderblocks for table legs, a 6 x 3-foot piece of plywood for the desktop, a draftsman's lamp that clamped onto the table, a bookstand meant to hold a dictionary and lastly an office chair. You take those ingredients, add books to an eager and industrious mind, stir gently don't shake, and you can manufacture a medical student capable of achieving 87th percentile results on the National Boards.

There were generally two types of students. Those that intended to become competent practitioners through diligent study and a lifetime of learning and those who looked for angles to finagle their way through if they could. One of those angles appeared quickly.

All the students had to take human anatomy in their first semester. Between the stink of the formaldehyde and the hideous sight of previously worked-on cadaver specimens being brought to your examining table like an entree each day, the experience of anatomy class was rattling. It was very hard to resist the desensitization process that was natural under these circumstances. You became comfortable with the ghoulish. You sought and found humor in this bizarre atmosphere. The word got out that if you supplied a human skeleton to the anatomy department your grade in the course would benefit.

So began the bone rush of '72.

My friend Matt told me his tale of intrigue. He had two roommates and somehow they had made a connection with a local cemetery through a shady back-channel deal. They drove over to the graveyard past the headstones, far to the back and to the right. They parked at the designated spot. They could see dirt flying out of a deep hole but the grave digger was too deep to be visible. One of the boys approached the rim of the grave, leaned over the edge and said something. In short order, a man emerged from his digging, walked over to a nearby headstone and from behind it he retrieved a cement bag that was waiting there. After the brief exchange of a few hundred pesos, the boys were back on the road with their prize, full of anticipation and anxious to view their purchase.

They lived in a typical rented stucco home that had an enclosed patio behind the house. On the wall of the patio was a metal double sink. It was the perfect place to examine the contents of the bag.

Out tumbled a human skull and the full complement of a disarticulated skeleton. True it was creepy but it also seemed funny in a macabre way. They began to realize how desensitized they had become in such short order. Little thought was given to the identity of the deceased. The sacrilege of disturbing the dead was oddly not very repulsive. They began to wash the specimen with detachment as it was quite dirty. They left it in the sink to soak in Clorox.

Now Matt's landlord had an unusual son. He was a handsome 19-year-old with a blond beard and long dirty blond hair that hung down his back below his shoulder blades. He was always in brown leather sandals and wore all white clothes. There was a large golden crucifix with the body of the Savior on a chain around his neck and he was said to be very religious. He was also a deaf mute. Overall, he gave the appearance of a very quiet Jesus walking amongst us.

He picked a very bad time to wander into the patio. When he saw the gleaming skull in the sink he let out an unintelligible guttural sound, crossed himself repeatedly and fled the scene with pupils dilated in a panic. The boys never saw him again and oddly never heard a word about it from the landlord. They did duly donate the skeleton to the anatomy department where it was accepted with gratitude.

Whether it helped anyone to get a better grade or not remains a mystery.

There were some fine instructors on the faculty. The anatomy department head, Dr Lopez Martinez, stood out. He was very energetic and had a genius for teaching. He could instruct at a rapid speed while drawing intricate anatomical illustrations with colored chalk on a blackboard using both hands simultaneously. It would look like Frank Netter, MD himself had drawn it right before your eyes. To me, Doctor Netter was the Norman Rockwell of anatomical drawing.

The real studying though happened in your room. You read textbooks and committed unbelievable amounts of detailed scientific information into your permanent memory. For the first time in my academic career I was creating an organized corpus of knowledge. Each subject dovetailed into the next so that a solid base could be constructed with all the pieces interconnecting.

Until then, education had seemed like a process of throwing disorganized information into a storage bin for later use. Like most closets, much of its contents would lie in wait indefinitely, waiting to be pulled out and used someday were it to find a use.

The amassing of an integrated body of knowledge was a major discovery for me. Though I had preferred the study of the humanities rather than science, I became fascinated with the mechanics of the human body as taught in physiology. Biochemistry explained the miracle of metabolism. Embryology traced the transformation from sperm and egg to a full human infant, differentiated into male and female outcomes from the same basic materials with just a slight genetic twist, a Y rather than an X chromosome was all that was required for that magic.

Pharmacology was a vital key and opened the toolbox that science had provided for the modern healer. Microbiology defined the invisible enemies that caused infection. Histology demonstrated the microscopic structure of the different tissues of the body. Pathology taught the catalogue of effects caused by the myriad maladies that afflicted humanity.

It turned out that the academic material taught in class was far exceeded by my own schedule of reading. I didn't know exactly how much I needed to learn to achieve my goals so I read everything I could endure. At least eight hours and often many more, were spent every day in this endeavor, long into the blurry-eyed zone.

We were required to attend all lectures and a roll call was taken before every class. The instructor would call out your name, first your father's last name, then your mother's maiden name, then your first name and finally your middle name. You were then required to respond with "Presente".

Of course the lecture was delivered in Spanish and since I was far ahead of the class through my own studies, I would have a lot of free mental time on my hands. On cool mornings, I would wear my serape to class. With my head stuck out through the hole I would imagine I was still in bed under the covers, not yet quite ready to get up. In the two years I spent there I only got busted for snoring once.

There were many wonderful experiences during those two years, trips to Puerto Vallarta, camping on the beach, homemade music so beautiful that it made your heart swell. It was a most engaging time.

Your friends were all in the same boat and we felt very tightly bound together.

However, you had to be careful. Though life usually proceeded peacefully, you had to watch your step. There was a common perception that if somehow you were dragged into the netherworld of the Mexican legal system, you might disappear into some unpleasant chasm from which only a large bribe from home might secure your freedom. This heightened my awareness yet again how precious our American civil liberties were and how easy it was to take them for granted. By the end of two years, everyone I knew was anxious to transfer back and end their Mexican adventure.

CHAPTER 23

The Butterfly Emerges

I REMEMBER THE DAY that I realized I had a singular role model. It was a sudden yet subtle transformation and the circumstances were quite odd. It was a beautiful early afternoon in Guadalajara. The previous evening I had seen the movie *Doctor Zhivago* again for the third time in my life. It was shown in a downtown cinema that had vestiges of a glorious past. It was a very spacious theater with a sea of seats. As you waited for the show to begin the low lights revealed the skyline of a city along the side walls. The black backlit silhouettes of buildings left the impression of a bygone era of big dreams. The thinness of the audience scattered around in the seats suggested a different reality.

The show began and I was moved in a way that I had never been before. It was everything you might hope a film could do for you. It left a much stronger impression, a turbulence of meaning much more powerful than it had ever done in the past. After all, now I was a medical student. I had dabbled in writing poetry and I related to Yuri's romantic embrace of life. But what lay ahead for me still remained an abstraction. It would take years of reflection and experience to fully understand the transformative power of viewing that film at that precise time in my life. I had a vague idea of what being a doctor would actually be like, but it seemed so theoretical. Would I even enjoy the reality of such a life? Did I really have what it took? For the present I was absorbed by the need to stay attentive to what lay immediately before me. At least I had a focused purpose, a pathway to follow. It was an act of faith.

This is what I was thinking about that sunny afternoon. Wearing a T shirt, comfortable khaki shorts and sandals, I was walking my beloved Blacky whom I had taken back down to the Guad on my last trip home. I was playing a lousy rendition of the Eagle's *Desperado* on my brown plastic recorder with heartfelt emotion while I walked. As I passed a construction site, a worker whistled at me. Now, I knew he wasn't admiring my legs. No, he was mocking me. He was letting me know that real men don't wear shorts, not in his Mexico, especially not blowing on a whistle and walking like that down a public street. It seemed to offend his sense of machismo. He was conveying a challenge to me. I could feel his taunt: "I see you and I'm calling you out, that's right just keep walking, what are you going to do about it? "

Well, anyway that is what I thought he was saying with that whistling crap. Apparently, I was violating his sense of public decency. I had no interest in addressing his affront to my manhood. After all, I was a guest in his country. A response would be pointless. The situation was a distraction from the reverie I was having. But I recovered quickly from this intrusion of negativity. A smile quickly reemerged and my spirit again began to flow nicely as I headed on down the street to the park at the end of the road.

The bad but soulful flute music resumed.

Now Blacky was a large tricolor collie with a proud and prominent chest that was endowed with plentiful thick white hair. That chest was accentuated by the contrast of the black and brown coloration over the rest of his magnificent frame and his handsome face. He gave you confidence wherever you might walk with him.

He was famous for calmly approaching the dogs he would encounter in his path, walk up to them with that big chest puffed out like a ramming prow of a war ship and press it into the side of said new dog on the block. He always held high his proud head and white tipped tail at such a moment.

I had never seen the object of his investigation fail to back down and let him proceed with his calm examination of the canine stranger. Sometimes there would be a bit of fighting but mainly only to allow the other dog to escape. More often there would be eventual tail wagging and the mutual smelling of assholes.

I let the big boy off his leash when we entered the park. The coast was clear and we had the park to ourselves, or so I thought. Several minutes later a fearful sight appeared at the other entrance. It was a very large and scary looking Doberman. He was loose and alone. That breed is famous for its ferocity and was a common choice as a guard dog in Guadalajara.

This one had a mean and hungry look. He appeared to have been living on the streets for a while, no collar, scruffy and lean. As the elements of this drama began to dawn on me, Blacky started his typical chest out approach.

"Oh shit," I thought, "this was not going to end well."

The Dobie stood his ground, completely unimpressed by the Black Man's posture. He just fixed an unnerving stare upon my dear dog and my heart started to race. I picked up a brick that was lying on the ground with the intention of bashing in the brains of the stray once the fur started to fly. But then a miracle happened. Blacky walked past the Dobie as if he wasn't there and that nasty beast just let him go on his way. I had never seen Blacky do that before.

Dum de dum de dum he calmly headed for the park exit and I dropped the brick. With an intense sense of relief I followed him out onto the street. The Dobie just stood there looking. Now that was some brilliant canine insight on my dog's part. You had to admire him, his timing was superb. Ole', I thought. Blacky you are truly a matador.

Well, I hooked up his leash, settled down a bit and we continued on our walk. I started to reflect again on Zhivago's character and how the film had affected me so deeply the night before. I find it interesting, almost fifty years later, that I still vividly recall the cascade of events as they unfolded that day. I can't say that the odd experiences on my walk represented anything more than a random assortment of challenging distractions. That is just how the day played out. But by the time I reached my doorstep I sensed that a profound spiritual transformation was underway. From that day forward I felt a bond, a kindredness with Yuri Zhivago that has endured to the present. It was the movie that had been the trigger. I had reached a critical turning point in my life and for that I am most grateful.

CHAPTER 24

Another Door Opens.

AFTER THE SECOND-YEAR EXAMS were over at the *Universidad Autonoma de Guadalajara*, I packed up Blacky and all my belongings and loaded them into my car. I was not planning on coming back to Mexico, but in truth I might have to haul it all back down again in the Fall if I failed in my attempt to transfer. No sense worrying about that now. The task at hand was to get home and take the Med Boards. My applications were already submitted to several schools. Once the test results were known, the American med schools would fill any vacancies in their programs. These open slots would appear when people dropped out or if the class expanded for its clinical phase.

That is where the foreign medical students fit in.

The day of the Med Boards arrived and I settled into a seat. Strangely the test was being given in a movie theater in North Jersey. The competition was about to begin. It felt partly like a lottery, partly like a wrestling match. I was raring to go at the gate, ready for the challenge, give me that number 2 pencil, let's go!!

It was a beautiful thing. I knew the material cold. The advice that had been given to me on how to prepare for this contest was uncannily accurate. Leaving the exam hall I felt confident, but I still had three weeks to wait for results.

Then my phone rang.

I was invited for an interview at New Jersey Medical School in Newark. I was accepted..

Vindication. Validation. Elation and a definite prayer of thanks. I wouldn't have to drive all the way down south this coming Fall after all.

CHAPTER 25

Free Fallin'

I CAN'T SAY THAT all my dreams suddenly came true, but I had been mightily blessed. The cascade of events in each life pours out in its own sequence with innumerable turning points and no one should be considered lucky until their last breath is taken, so the ancients had pointed out.

I had the expectation that I would be entering the hallowed halls of learning to experience an accelerated and sophisticated teaching method. I wasn't prepared for the reality before me. The old Martland Hospital in Newark became the locus of my new academic world. It was a gritty inner city teaching hospital in a rough and tumble urban landscape full of danger and decay. The patients coming through the doors were often bitter and disillusioned. Pervasive poverty and street violence impacted most of the life stories of the sick and injured that came for their care at that outdated facility. It was an exposure to a sense of hopelessness I had not experienced before and it had a sobering effect. These situations were no longer just someone else's problems, I was now a witness, a participant in the drama all around me.

The neighborhood was unsafe to enter and leave, particularly at night, though everyone working there seemed to ignore this obvious situation much to their credit. The oddness of my new environment would eventually diminish and become almost normal. It was conducive to good mental health to adapt and move on. But the irony of missing the relative calm and comfort of my time spent in Guadalajara was not lost on me.

Watch out for what you wish for, as the old saw goes.

The basic teaching unit in the clinical years is the medical team. It consists of medical students, interns, resident physicians and the attending physician. It is a traditional method which has produced generation after generation of fine practitioners. It often provides excellent health care to the nation's indigent, though far from solving the health care deficits in that neglected segment of society. This offered a compelling challenge to give comfort to the neediest in our country and to make your interventions as fruitful as possible. That indeed is an important insight to remember and master.

The faults of the physician training regimen are often mistakenly thought to be the keys to its success. The crazy long hours, the uncontrolled workload, the lack of sleep during busy night sessions followed by a full working schedule the next day, the abysmally low salary of the residents (the medical students, of course, paid tuition for the privilege of their education), the stage is set on the hospital wards to condition the acolyte to function under these conditions and to normalize these unpleasantries.

I am still not convinced that this level of stress improves the ideal final product, a compassionate and competent practitioner. I don't believe that sheer volume, variety and repetition are so important that they justify this marathon process to which the initiate is subjected. It always seemed to me that this system was as much a source of providing cheap labor to deliver very expensive care as it was a time-tested teaching environment. It wasn't all charity. Someone was doing the billing, someone was collecting and we were doing the work.

Thus, the training regimen was built on the traditional view that working through sleep deprivation with lives depending on your acuity would build some sort of skill and stamina for an unknown future deluge of work. Certainly, there would be situations like that at times and it did train me to bolt upright in bed with a clear head when awakened at night. I don't think I possessed that skill before and it did prove to be a very useful skill when I had my own practice to manage.

Sadly, the nation would require a medical corps that could withstand punishing work volumes and ridiculously long hours for indefinite periods of time when the pandemic of 2019 arrived, but that was to be many years in the future.

I don't wish to sound unappreciative. Beggars can't be choosers. I do sincerely thank the citizens of the State of New Jersey for the chance they gave me. I would do it all over again but it was no walk in the proverbial park.

I had expected to receive focused bedside clinical teaching but basically you learned by following the clinical team and observing how they worked up and cared for the patients. You learned what you could at the bedside as the endless work progressed. You read all you could. I found this somewhat disorienting and I was surprised that

I felt that way. I had just finished two years of proving that I could learn very efficiently by just sitting alone in a room with a book.

Somehow finding myself thrown onto the medical ward in these unfamiliar surroundings had an inhibiting effect and I started to feel a strange sense of detachment. It took a number of months for me to acclimate myself and get comfortable with being there. All that fish out of water feeling came as a sobering surprise. My lavish expectations for life after transfer turned out to be a misinformed fantasy. It took some time to recover and get on properly with the task at hand.

It didn't help that I was living at home. On the positive side, I got to see my family every day and the distance was commutable. On the other hand, having a 25-year-old single male living in the house again made waves. As my mother pointed out, I had a thirteen-year-old brother at home and he was not ready to witness the kind of social life I was eager to engage in. I needed a place of my own to entertain properly, so to speak.

I got lucky. One day I saw a piece of paper on a bulletin board in the med school library. That is how I found two great second year med students who were looking for a roommate to share their apartment in West Orange. Charlie and Jerry became close and beloved friends and likely saved me from severe depression.

When I had transferred back, I no longer had a support group of friends. Thinking about it, I had passed through several cycles of peer groups....high school, college, Europe, Mexico and now back to New Jersey. After each phase I had had to sever bonds with friends and reestablish new ones as we all moved on. I again realized how comfortable I had been meeting people on the road and how difficult it had become for me to continue doing so at home.

I was no longer a member of a group of compatriots other than my fellow students and we were too busy and separated to offer much company and support to each other. It resulted in a sudden and profound sense of loneliness and alienation. Perhaps people were open on the road and closed off at home because at home they already had their circle of friends and family surrounding them. The context of their lives was laid out in patterns that didn't require the admittance of a new face. On the street people seemed wary of strangers and eye contact was often not welcome. I suppose this tendency can be overcome with a gregarious extroverted approach, the Billy Bleach method if you will. But I was discovering that I had become shy and put off by the lack of interest I seemed to arouse in others. Suddenly I was living in Lonely Town in a world overflowing with people. I met a few sweet ladies, and I thank them all, but I was not making that special connection, not finding the soulmate that a man of that age is ready to meet.

There were nights when I longed for that special lady. I began to think more and more about Alison. Where was she now? What was she doing? Was she still with Pierre? Married? Happy?

It had been over three years since we had said goodbye in Athens and we had not communicated since. I didn't know her address or her phone number. It was December and the Christmas break had come. I impulsively decided to hit the road and try to find her.

It was a wild long shot and a damn long ride to Canada. I was driving an old '65 Ford mustang hardtop that my friend Fred had sold me for $200. It was a little rusted out. You could lift up the back bumper and the body would separate from the chassis, but it ran like a top and the heater still worked. I packed some warm clothes and headed up to the Frozen North alone.

Montreal is very cold that time of year but it was refreshing to check out the well-dressed ladies in their stylish long leather coats and boots browsing at the downtown shops. The authentic French onion soup was delicious. The snow cover was more than a foot deep everywhere. I enjoyed my overnight stay in Montreal but no Alison McMaster could be found in the phone book.

The next morning, I drove up to Ottawa. When I got into town I found a phone booth. Steam formed with each breath as I closed the folding door, grabbed the phone book and, lo and behold, I found the name A. McMaster listed. Wow wouldn't that be something. I dialed the number and a lady answered. I introduced myself explaining that I was Alison's friend from Greece and had stopped by to say hello (this was a considerable understatement).

"Oh yes,", she said. "Alison is my daughter and she told me all about you when she came home. She'll be glad to hear from you. She's working at an agency called The Gray Goose."

She gave me the address and I drove over to the office, climbed the outdoor staircase to the second floor in a bound and knocked on the door. It had a picture of a gray Canadian goose painted on it. A nice lady opened the door and told me that Alison had left early that day and she was at her apartment. I asked if I could use their phone and call her. She kindly complied and suddenly there I was on the phone with the lovely Alison!

This was too good to be believed.

She was very excited to hear from me and said to come right over. I found her apartment, adjusted my Greek fisherman's hat and knocked on the door. She opened it and I was stunned. She was drop dead gorgeous and she had filled out nicely in all the right places. We fell upon each other in a passionate frenzy and afterwards we lay naked in bed smiling.

It was time to talk. We had hardly said a word since I came through the door.

I was ready to take her home with me, move her into my room, pick things up where we had left off in Greece. It seemed like no time had passed since I had last seen her. My heart was soaring like a hawk. But alas, she broke the news that she was actually on her way to Montreal to spend a few weeks with Pierre and his family. She couldn't cancel, she said, they were too involved and she was already late getting there.

"Come back with me," I said.

"I'm really tempted, but I can't. You can stay here as long as you'd like, just let yourself out." She kissed me sweetly.

Soon she was gone.

And with that Alison walked out of my life for good.

I was left feeling confused and very alone. It was nearly a miracle that I had actually found her and had the pleasure of her company. But the harsh reality that her door had closed permanently behind her left me feeling acutely abandoned....abandoned in Ottawa in the middle of winter no less.

As I left her place and followed the frozen stream that ran along her snow-covered road, I thought again about Joni Mitchell and this time her song *River* played in my head:

"It's coming on Christmas
They're cutting down trees
Their putting up reindeer
And singing songs of joy and peace

Oh I wish I had a river I could skate away on.
Oh I wish I had a river so long
I would teach my feet to fly
I wish I had a river
I could skate away on
I made my baby say goodbye."

IT WAS AN APPROPRIATE choice for a mental soundtrack. It suited the sad moment just right. But it only intensified the pain. It reminded me too much of the night she had left Athens when I had sat at the Carolina Hotel bar alone and drank her off my mind with that nasty tasting ouzo.

I limped home. It was a long, lonely ass ride.

CHAPTER 26

Climbing Back

GETTING BACK TO NEW Jersey, I struggled to get my head on straight. In time I got accustomed to the routine on the wards and began to thrive again. Learning the skills of physical diagnosis, history taking, interpreting test results, learning how to write orders and perform procedures, how to actually run cases, all this required a whole new set of skills. It was a challenge but also a gratifying opportunity to put into action all the scientific elements you had mastered in the classroom.

The thought about how much you still didn't know could be terrifying, so I chose not to think about it. Case by case you learned everything relevant to the treatment of whatever malady presented itself, from colds to cancer to heart attacks. Over time you began to accumulate the experience you would need when you were finally granted an unrestricted license to apply your own judgement. That judgement had better be excellent, lives would be in your hands. The mission took on a dire sense of reality that had, until so recently, been a theoretical exercise. Like combat, this immersion is an abruptly sobering experience. The trick was to emerge from the process with the skills and confidence to flourish in that arena without being intimidated by the challenge.

It was the time to learn the art of listening. It was an opportunity to discover the satisfaction that the alleviation of suffering brings. I began to learn how to flash into someone's life and within minutes grasp the essence of their conflicts and struggles. While you assessed the physical basis of their complaints and formulated a diagnostic and therapeutic plan, it was important to understand the unique spiritual nature and qualities of the person who entrusted their care to you. This created the opportunity to form a special bond with complete strangers, tight connections formed within minutes that were so rare to develop when meeting people outside the context of your exam room. This was the area in the practice of medicine that offered the most poetic possibilities. The patients greatly appreciated the contact and the concern as you weathered crises with them and their families.

I found that if you strived to give more than was necessary, you would be rewarded with good results and gratitude. No one is infallible, we all make errors but it is important not to make mistakes because of laziness, greed or inattentiveness. These seemingly simple maxims are the type of lessons that build one's character, something beyond simply achieving scientific competence. Yes, it is hard work. Medicine is a cruel mistress. It can surely break you down and burn you out. Yet it is a fantastic opportunity to learn about being a human being, to fight the good fight against pain and disease, to soothe souls. To be a scientific shaman, a poet physician.

I had a few pleasant breaks during my last year of medical school. We were able to take work assignments while still students at outside institutions, what they called externships. I spent two months with a family practice group in rural Maine and six weeks in Honolulu at the city's pediatric hospital.

Hawaii was not hard to take. The staff and people I met there were very friendly and welcoming. They were surprised I was from the New York metropolitan area. I seemed oddly mellow compared to others they had run into from my old stomping grounds. I took that as a sign of success and a product of my years of traveling. I was invited to a local home for a Hawaiian Thanksgiving with smoked turkey cooked in a steel drum, served with poi and Kailua pig to accompany the pumpkin pie and stuffing.

There was a pediatric resident who would joke with me and tell me about a recurring nightmare he kept having. In it he was on call for the ER and there was a Samoan skateboard contest. Apparently the Samoans were very accident prone. I really couldn't comment on the appropriateness of this joke but I laughed every time he said it, he was a damn funny guy.

Finally, back in New Jersey, it was graduation day and a very proud moment for my parents. We were handed our diplomas, took the Hippocratic Oath in unison as a class and obtained the prized MD that was now ours for life. Of course, it was just the beginning. I was scheduled to start my residency in Family Practice in a hospital on Long Island. The thought that I would now be running the show was daunting. Did I really have what it took?

CHAPTER 27

Doctor Man Emerges
From The Elevator

IT'S A STRANGE THING. Maybe it was the beeper, maybe the white coat hanging down to my mid thighs with the Washington Manual secured in one pocket and my stethoscope curled up in another. I'm not sure exactly how it happened, but I got into the elevator on the ground floor as a worried young man, a new resident at South Side Hospital, and by the time I reached the third floor Medical Ward I felt I had undergone a transformation.

I emerged from the elevator and somehow I knew I was really a doctor. I never looked back. A miraculous confidence seemed to fill my being and I knew I was ready and eager for the challenge of my life. I had no further doubts about my readiness to assume my duties and I dove right in. How this transformation took place on an elevator ride remains a mystery.

As the weeks and months rolled by, my confidence and competence grew and I began to flourish. Working the ER, OB, the

Neonatal Unit, the Intensive Care Unit, I became comfortable with treating the sickest patients in conjunction with an array of specialists, resident physicians and attending physicians. We assisted in surgeries, delivered babies, learned the basics of orthopedics and all the specialty areas.

By the third year you were a senior resident, teaching the residents in the years behind you. By June of 1979 I was ready to strike out on my own. I felt well prepared to enter private practice. But I was lonely. I hadn't found *that* girl, at least not until the last days of my training when I was almost out the door. That is when I happened to meet Lisa completely by chance.

How is that for luck?

CHAPTER 28

Go West Young Man

As I TOLD YOU in the beginning of this saga, Lisa and I split for the West Coast soon after I finished my residency. The immediate intensity of our relationship was breathtaking and had been totally unforeseen. Our futures beckoned brightly before us. We were so excited to be together and we were more than ready to leave the area.

As it turned out, we would rarely see the Northeast again.

We averaged about 600 miles a day, switching drivers to keep moving when one of us grew tired, looking for a campground to pitch our tent each night and to catch some sleep.

The ride out to Colorado was uneventful. We thought we might stay and make a go of it out there but the rural areas we had in mind seemed a little too challenging considering the deep snows we could expect in the winter and the frequent commuting to a hospital at all hours. So we decided to take in the sights. We had especially wanted to see the famous frontier town turned celebrity ski haven, Telluride.

It was mid-August when we left Denver and took Route 70 to Grand Junction. The route was scenic enough but we were saving the spectacular ride for the day we would leave Telluride and head down the famous Million Dollar Highway. This is a gut-wrenching collection of high altitude twist and turns through incredible vistas of forests and river. It runs 25 miles from Silverton through the beautiful old West railroad town of Ouray and finally hits the low country at Dolores on the New Mexico border.

The sights are best left to the passenger because the driver has to contend with white knuckle corners with their long drops into the valleys below. Many a driver has plunged to their death into that alluring backdrop.

The road into Telluride was a lot tamer but still a lovely ride. We pulled into a campground on the outskirts of town at around 4 PM. We were lucky to find a spot. It was still the height of tourist season and we didn't have a reservation. There was one tent site still available and soon our tent was up. Lisa blew up the air mattress. It turned out that she was the one with the lungs in the family. She had been a competitive swimmer in high school.

I started a fire in the stone fire ring and Lisa was rustling up dinner. It was a beautiful scene with the sunset just coming on and the rose colored clouds darkening by the minute. I always loved the drama of the colors at that time of day. Time seemed so much more dynamic when the changes were swift.

I grabbed my guitar and started a shitty rendition of the Eagles' *Peaceful Easy Feeling*. I could barely carry a tune and the guitar work was sad but it was homemade music and I think Lisa enjoyed it. I was getting into it when a guy showed up unannounced with his guitar, sits down next to me and starts riffing. I'll give it to him. He had some talent.

Now I'm not too happy about this development. First of all, I have no idea who he is and secondly, I'm in the process of wooing the object of my affection. After all, we had only been together for about six weeks. It felt like it would last forever to me but, you never know. I was in no mood to be taking chances.

After the song ended, the guy pipes up. "Hi, name's Joe."

He had long stringy dirty blond hair, a beard and mustache and was wearing a flannel shirt and faded blue jeans. He seemed quite taken with himself. I was liking him less.

"Hi", said Lisa, apparently I was the only one with my antennae up

Well, Joe started in on an acoustic solo. He was pretty good but I was getting less and less amused. After a few interminable minutes of his entertaining I said, "OK Joe, we're getting ready for dinner."

He looked at me a little surprised at the sudden turn in the conversation. Apparently he was used to encores, not to getting the hook. It looked like he couldn't tell if this was an invitation to eat with us or if he was getting his plug pulled. I shot him a look that took the guesswork out of the situation.

"You know, two years ago a couple was hiking in the woods around here. They went missing and a few days later their bodies turned up. They never found the guy who did it." said Joe out of nowhere.

"Thanks for the local color." I said.

With that he got up and slipped out of our camp.

"That was kind of creepy." said Lisa.

"Let's eat, Darlin'."

The next morning I woke up to find Lisa already outside the tent and busy. She was always the early riser in the family. Down by a little creek brushing her teeth, she was wearing a pair of blue jean overalls and facing away from me. Her beautiful auburn hair cascaded to the small of her back. I stood there for a minute just taking it all in.

She was using that magic liquid, Dr Bronner's to brush her teeth. It was that stuff with the nice peppermint flavor that she used for everything from toothpaste to laundry detergent. Getting with the program, I had already moved on from Crest toothpaste and was a Bronner advocate myself. It was little things that drew you together, helped to seal the deal.

"You look damn good in the morning."

"Thank you, kind sir." She said.

"You in the mood for breakfast?'

"Definitely!" was the answer.

We got organized and headed into Telluride. It had retained enough of its gold mining Old West flavor that you could imagine a movie set with Butch Cassidy robbing the local bank. A feat he actually accomplished in 1888. The town had morphed into a trendy ski resort and the feel of St Moritz was also palpable. It made for an interesting upscale amalgam and was very Colorado. We ducked into a little breakfast place on the main street.

The waitress seated us in a quiet corner booth and we ordered some coffee and omelets. I was stirring in the sugar and cream and happened to look up. In through the door walked Joe the guitar player.

He didn't look our way and I don't think Lisa noticed . She was sitting facing away from him. He sat at the counter and nursed his coffee and bagel. I only saw him turn our way once as he adjusted himself in his seat.

I tried not to concern myself with his presence but I have to say the scene made me a bit uneasy and I kept an eye on him. We finished our meal, paid at the table and left a nice tip. He didn't turn around as we walked by the counter to leave the restaurant.

When we were outside I asked Lisa, "Did you see the campground Romeo?'

"Who?"

"Joe. He was sitting at the counter,"

"I didn't see him." she said. "It's a small town I guess."

"Maybe a little too small for my liking. C'mon, let's check the place out."

We spent a few hours walking around town. It is a beautiful place with towering mountains in the short distance visible at the end of the main street. Indeed the town is enveloped by mountains thick with pine and fir forests.

I had heard about a hot spring near town nestled in the woods with a collection of famous hot tubs you could hire for a dip. It was a favorite haunt of the hippies that had flocked to the area in the late 60's. Now that sounded like a fine afternoon destination so we headed off to find the place. My friend in Denver had given us very precise directions and we parked the car at the trail head just over an old wooden bridge.

The trail was narrow but clearly marked and we walked for what seemed to be at least a mile. We didn't encounter a soul and I started to get a bit uneasy, wishing I had a pistol. There was total silence and I wondered if we were indeed on the right trail. Lisa looked unconcerned and eager for adventure. Finally, we came into a clearing and saw a stand of old run down wooden cabins. Not a soul in sight. Apparently we had arrived a few years late to join the party. The spring was there but no hot tubs.

I felt a sudden combination of disappointment and exposure.

"Let's head back, what do you say?"

"OK, not much here." She said'.

I lead the way back up the trailhead at a little faster pace than we had come down. It was a relief to see the car and even better to get back to the campsite, our little home sweet home. We relaxed and settled in for the evening.

The next morning we packed our gear and decided to hit the Million Dollar Highway. It was a gorgeous day with a cloudless sky. There was only one road out of town and the traffic was slow and heavy. We saw a Western outfitter store on the left and pulled in to have a look. They had a real nice assortment of leather goods, saddles, boots and Zuni jewelry. I was studiously shopping the jewelry counter looking for just the right ring to buy my lovely lady when I glanced up and caught sight of Joe.

It dawned on me that this was no coincidence. Our car, being a bright blue Triumph convertible, was easy to track and this creep was stalking us.

"Time to go." I nudged Lisa and she caught sight of him.

There was no telling what his intentions were or if he was armed. I had no intention of trying to find out. Lisa caught my vibe and we quickly made our way to the car and pulled into traffic.

Unfortunately, we joined a several mile long traffic jam. It was Sunday morning and the weekend tourists all had the same idea. The main hang-up was a series of traffic lights that kept us inching forward at a crawl.

Lisa turned and looked back, "He's in a pickup three cars behind us!"

"Shit, we just gotta' wait out this traffic."

It was a good twenty minutes until we came to the last light. The road was clear ahead after that and I timed the light so that I got through the yellow and left old Joe three cars back waiting for the green. This was my chance and I gunned the engine, racing off toward Silverton and the roller coaster I knew lay ahead.

I drove as fast as I could, which was easy at first until we started climbing high into the mountains and negotiating hairpin turns without guardrails. I didn't let up for a minute, sweating and scaring the hell out of myself more than once. I couldn't take my eyes off the road for a second, so Lisa kept watch out to our rear.

"Do you see that bastard, honey?"

"No, it's still clear."

And that's the way it went all the way to the flats in Dolores. I never have gotten to see Ouray, it was just a flash we passed by on the highway.

I still didn't see Joe's truck but I thought better than to stop in this first town, we might be too easy to spot. So I drove another ten miles before pulling into a motel. I parked way around the back so the car wasn't visible from the road and we checked in.

It was an uneasy night, but that was the end of the drama. No Joe.

"What do you say we head out for California?"

"Sounds like a plan." Said my beautiful companion.

Route 80 runs from New York City to San Francisco. When you finally reach the end of the desert near Reno you can see the Sierra Nevada rising up. It's a beautiful sight.

I said to Lisa, "Over those mountains lies our destiny."

I felt the grandeur of that thought and I reveled in the freedom of not knowing what the hell our destiny would be. There were no thoughts of failure, more a naive confidence that everything was about to fall into place. That is a rare and wonderful situation to find yourself in. And besides, Lake Tahoe was just up the road.

CHAPTER 29

The Scalpel's Edge

MY MUFFLER HAD FALLEN off on the ascent from Reno but that didn't deter us, we just strapped it onto the tiny luggage rack of the Triumph and kept rolling loudly until we could find a mechanic.

We spent a delightful week resting at Lake Tahoe. We had driven from Colorado without much of a break and the respite was glorious. Tahoe is a wonderland of mountain, forests of pine and the majestic lake. There is skiing in the winter and boating in the summer. Here you could pitch your tent at a campground and at night you could see BB King perform in the intimate yet casual setting of Harrah's Casino.

Well. we were out West, so now what? It was clear we needed to formulate a game plan as my borrowings from Chase Bank were dwindling. I did some research, made a few phone calls and hooked up a month-to-month gig working at Eureka General Hospital.

The car ride up to Eureka was beautiful and fascinating. We had left Lake Tahoe passing through the mountain forests that had trapped the starving Donner Party in the deep snows of that cannibal winter so long ago. Then we pressed on to Sacramento.

We stopped there for the night and got to visit with Lisa's step-grandfather, Mr. Champ Neville. He was an interesting old timer who hailed from Biloxi Mississippi. It was said that he got his start moonshining and may have run a whorehouse down there before World War I. He had married Lisa's Finnish Grandma, Gaga Vie as they called her. That was short for her given name Viena. They had divorced many years ago. It was said that the old gent had fought in France during the Great War in 1918. The story was told in the family that he would periodically return to France and could still find a French lady willing to share her bed with him for a pair of silk stockings. That seemed like a stretch to me but he was charming.

We all called him Papa Samps. He had met Gaga Vie in Miami where he ran a pawn shop. All that was ancient history now. He was well into his eighties but he had a certain Southern gentility about him. He introduced us to his current girlfriend Madge, a sweet quiet older lady.

We took Samps out for a lovely meal at the upscale steak house in Old Sac called D O Mills. It had a huge old bank vault in the lobby and the food was delicious. He loved every minute of it, especially when we drove him in our little Triumph and Lisa had to sit on his lap. It was a bit creepy but we could see how happy it made him.

The next morning, we headed up north, passing through San Francisco and up over the Golden Gate Bridge to enter the natural wonderland that awaited us. It's a good eight hour drive from San Francisco to Eureka. There are plenty of wonderful places to check on the way. We particularly liked Mendocino on the ocean and had a fine dinner there. Garberville made for an interesting stop. This was a town where homes were bought in cash long before their crop of fine sinsemilla was legal.

Eureka ,California is a fairly large, picturesque town in a remote area of Northern California. It is set in one of the most naturally beautiful areas of America, but what was that smell in the air?

It was hard to describe exactly, but once you experienced it you would never confuse it with another odor. Locals told me it was the smell of money. It was something I had never smelled before and it was not at all pleasant, sort of a mustache on this otherwise lovely lady of a Victorian town. A town set on a Pacific bay where primordial forests of gigantic redwood trees had once stood unmolested for eons.

The omnipresent stink was spewing from pulp mills that still were processing local timber. Some of the noble redwood giants remained, protected by law or by the generosity of private foundations like the Save The Redwoods League. Those dedicated and forward-looking souls had bought up extensive tracts of land before all the ancient giants could succumb to the voracious saws. These towering survivors had been young trees when Jesus walked upon the earth, expressions of nature's power and beauty that had resisted all challenges. They had defied age itself.

We had driven up to this corner of Humboldt County for my first real job since finishing residency. I would be working at the Hospital with a small crew of Family Practitioners covering the ER, a walk-in clinic and an inpatient service. I was excited at the offer which was paying me a real salary for the first time in my life, instead of the pittance I received for my arduous labors as a resident physician.

After we got into town, we rented a dumpy little third story apartment in an old house that sat across the street from a public auditorium. I would occasionally serve as ringside doctor at boxing matches held in that building to generate a little extra income. I settled in at the hospital and got to work. It was hectic but I was used to all kinds of stresses and our time passed quickly over the ensuing few months as we accumulated some scratch to replenish our dwindling cash reserves. We considered living in Eureka but first we wanted to check out permanent employment opportunities in northern California and Oregon.

We flew Blacky in from Florida by plane and bought a small trailer to track behind our Triumph. We loaded up our gear and our dog and we headed out for our reconnaissance. We spent several weeks looking far and wide but nothing seemed to be a fit. Our most interesting opportunity was in the town of Brookings on the southern coast of Oregon where it abuts the California state line.

Rusty Penny, MD was a local FP who wanted a partner. The setting was beautiful. This area of Oregon is known locally as the Banana Belt, famous for its temperate climate. Pristine rivers that once teemed with steelhead trout and salmon dotted the coast. It was rural with several local Indian reservations in the vicinity. Stands of old growth redwood giants still grew unmolested and protected just off the coast.

Doctor Penny and his charming wife Laurel lived on a beautiful patch of land along the banks of the narrow Winchuck River. He also owned a small house in the little town of Smith River just south of the California border and he was looking for a partner to help with that office and his main location in Brookings. I was seriously interested but in the end I decided I wanted a solo practice; somewhere I could establish the ideal practice I envisioned without having to accommodate a partnership.

It was with more than a bit of disappointment that we returned to Eureka to sort things out. I was frustrated at the lack of results on our journey.

At that point I impulsively said to Lisa,

"Let's go back East, it just doesn't feel like it's gonna work out here."

The day arrived when we planned to take off and head back whence we had come. We were walking out the door and I had our phone in my hand. I had removed it from the wall, planning to return it to the phone company and then immediately split East. You just can't get closer to out the door.

Lisa said, "Call Rusty before we go."

"He was a really nice guy, but I don't want a partner." said I.

"Call him anyway," she insisted.

"Ok," I said to humor her.

I placed the phone back on the wall and dialed Rusty.

"Hey Rusty, how you doing?"

"I'm fine, did you consider my offer?"

"I did and I really was tempted but I decided I want to practice solo."

"No problem," he said. "You can set up your own practice in Smith River. I'll rent the space to you and help you get started."

....

Put the phone back on the wall. How close can you get? And just like that we turned 180 degrees in our trajectory and embraced the life of a solo rural Family Practitioner in Smith River. That made me the most northern physician on the coast of California. You may wait and wait for Fate to declare itself to you but sometimes it just pops out of nowhere. Sometimes impulsiveness bordering on recklessness combines with opportunity and a spirit of flexibility to produce unexpected and wonderful life changes.

Sometimes you need to go with the flow.

CHAPTER 30

A Flag Is Planted

WE OPENED UP SHOP in a small three-bedroom house along Highway 101 North just south of the Oregon border. The population of the town was about 500 souls if you counted the residents of the nearby trailer park. With a few minor alterations we were up and running in no time. Lisa was my receptionist, medical assistant, you name it. Just the two of us and I was going to do it my way.

Lisa and I rented a two-bedroom single wide mobile home in the back of a mobile home dealership in Brookings Oregon and we settled in. That was our home for the first two lean years. We hadn't come out to the back country to make a fortune. We expected to be poor for quite a while.

I would not buy lab equipment or X ray capabilities. I could get lab tests much cheaper for my patients by drawing blood and sending it out to a commercial lab. X rays and urgent labs were available at the hospital when needed. I had no incentive to perform tests to pay off my equipment. I would order only what I needed to properly care for my patients.

I charged very low fees but I requested payment at the time. I thought of it in terms of John Arbuckle's famous maxim: "You get what you pay for" and I was determined to provide as much value as I could.

I was working for the patient, not their insurance company. I was on a mission to keep their costs as low as possible while still providing the very best care. It was the purest medical business model I was ever to encounter and it gave me a great sense of satisfaction.

Soon after we got to town, I went over to the local post office, a tiny building with a one room lobby. The postmaster introduced me in a friendly manner to Doctor Gilroy who was there picking up his mail.

He eyed me suspiciously and hesitated to shake my extended hand.

"No, no," said the Postmaster, "he's a people doctor."

Doctor Gilroy was relieved and he relaxed immediately. He was a veterinarian and when he realized I was not a competitor showing up unannounced in his little town, he was most amiable and we soon became good friends. It was my introduction to the intrigue of competition that tends to arise between fellow professionals. I was not by nature competitive and I had not come this great distance to entice people to leave their doctors and come to see me. I presumed there were unfulfilled needs in the community and I was here to offer my help.

Our little house of an office provided adequate working space to get started. We put a ramp out front and built a desk for reception. We got all the equipment I would need for the two exam rooms and the last bedroom became my consultation room. The dining room became our chart and lab area while the living room was a natural waiting room. There was nothing fancy about the office but the honesty and dedication to the mission came across loud and clear.

It was situated on a lot astride highway 101 which at that point was a two-lane country road. Across the way, hills studded with old growth redwood giants were arrayed. Occasionally, you could see big Roosevelt elk grazing up there with their broad antlers. Locals still panned for gold in the upriver riffles of the turquoise Smith River that flowed down through the little town and then, nearby, to the sea. One day a young man with a shotgun and a six pack of soda came in and introduced himself. It was a bit weird, but we accepted his gift. Fortunately, he proved to be harmless.

Not long after we arrived, my beloved dog Blacky, my faithful longtime companion who had shared so much with me over the years, that wandering guy, got hit by a truck on the highway in Brookings and was killed instantly.

This was very hard for me to take. I lifted his still warm body from the road, placed him in a large black plastic bag and brought him to my office. There was a small empty lot next to the office that was also owned by Dr Penney. I began digging a grave for my poor friend as darkness fell. I could still be near him that way.

I was in tears and really struggling to control my emotions. I became somewhat oblivious to my surroundings. Lisa touched me softly on my shoulder and said," You do realize you're digging a grave right next to a doctor's office, don't you?"

I looked up. Cars were passing slowly by in the night. It had not occurred to me that the motorists might wonder who or what the doctor was burying. The old adage "doctors bury their mistakes" crossed my mind and the black humor broke the tension.

I finished up and we sat down together to mourn on the steps of our little trailer. "Marry me Lisa, let's have some babies," I said.

She thought about it, smiled and said, "OK Honey."

Perhaps I should have picked a more romantic setting to propose such a momentous undertaking but she understood. She always understood.

Those years in Del Norte County provided many busy, wonderful days, and many very busy nights.

At that time, there were only five family practitioners and one general surgeon in the entire county. No other doctors. We each covered our own practices 24 hours a day, 7 days a week unless you could find a coverage partner. That could take quite a while for me to arrange at times.

There was only one hospital in the county, 15 miles from my office and 30 miles from my abode. It took some difficult juggling of time and distance but I made it work. We saw everything from heart attacks to gunshot wounds.

The doctors before me were legendary in the county. One of the old timer's had had a fatal car crash coming into the hospital one night. They named a beautiful bridge after him on Highway 199 at the site of the accident where it crossed the Smith River going up toward Hiouchi and Gasquet, the Doctor Fine bridge. That was long before my time.

There were some interesting rural legends that circulated. I heard a story about an episode in the ER quite a few years before my arrival. Electrical cardioversion for ventricular tachycardia, a potentially fatal heart rhythm, was just becoming recognized as a treatment for this calamity. The technique utilized electrical shocks of DC current applied directly to the chest. No such wonderful machine like that was yet available in small hospitals like ours. As the story went, the old country Doc cut a lamp cord and bared the wires, plugged the cord into the AC outlet, placed the wires across the patient's chest and bingo...no more ventricular tachycardia.

They say the man lived to go home and pick up the pieces of his almost severed life. Was this true or apocryphal? I have no idea. Fortunately, by the time I had arrived we had the proper DC defibrillators that we needed. But the fact remained that in such an isolated community, you sometimes had to be creative to obtain the best care for those who depended on you.

Emergency air service, Mercy Flights, was a godsend for the very ill who needed care in a large medical center. We would send the patients in small planes that took about 45 minutes to arrive at Rogue Valley Hospital in Medford Oregon. There a full complement of excellent specialists and the needed technologies were available. This usually ran without a hitch though there could be nerve wracking moments. On one sorrowful day, a mission of mercy ended in a plane crash and the death of all the brave souls aboard including the patient, pilot and medical team. Life and death were often the stakes and we fought the good fight in those days. I was very proud to be part of the healthcare system that served our county back then. The men and women, including all the nurses and other staff, were talented and very dedicated to the welfare of the community.

CHAPTER 31

A Cast Of Characters

THE MOST ENJOYABLE PART of my experience in the back country was meeting the memorable characters who entrusted me with their care. You will remember that I was born in 1949, only 89 years after the start of the American Civil War to give you some perspective. Just one full lifetime separated my existence from Pickett's charge at Gettysburg.

The older patients connected me with history in a very personal way. There was Nadine, a delightful older woman and a pharmacist, whose forebears had arrived from the Midwest in a Conestoga wagon settling in old Pasadena when it was still a little cow town.

There was the immaculately groomed diminutive British gentleman with his tidy, thin mustache, Mr. Richard Barker, who had been a fighter pilot for the RAF in the First World War. He was involved in a dog fight over France when his synchronized propeller failed to function properly. As he fired his machine gun, his propeller was shot to shreds and he made an emergency landing behind German lines. He was able to dodge and claw his way back to his own trenches and to safety. He was always well dressed and could have been cast in a 1940's World War II movie appearing as the senior British officer giving a briefing to a group of allied bomber pilots about to bomb a Nazi target in Germany. He was that cool, and I wondered how he wound up in my neck of the woods.

I recall the day his wife, whom he had instructed to stay in their car, came up to join him at our front desk. She was suffering from dementia though her sweet disposition always shone through. She had applied bright red lip stick but it tracked well beyond the borders of her lips. She was otherwise very neatly kempt. I smiled and said hello to her.

She said to me with obvious pride, "My first husband was a doctor you know"

Dick retorted, "Yes dear, he knows, and he got the best years of your mind."

The poignance of the moment struck me, the humor and the sorrow.

There was the irascible Rudy, a German U Boat captain during World War II. I can't remember many light moments between the two of us. But he did get the best care I could provide. Someone had given me a copy of *Mein Kampf* in German. I gave it to him and he seemed very excited. He never asked my opinion on the contents of that grotesque rant. The irony was definitely lost on him.

I had a definite tender spot for Joe Silver, a retired psychologist who suffered from depression. He had a lazy eye that I thought might have distracted his clients. He would ask me from time to time "How did you wind up in this sad ass town?" There were days when that question was not so easy to answer.

161

I made house calls back then for patients too frail to come to the office. You learned things in their homes that you might otherwise miss. The old-fashioned feelings engendered in performing this storied tradition still remains a cherished memory.

I was the only doctor for 15 miles in either direction. Sometimes I would have to intervene in urgent situations before the EMS could arrive. Occasionally I was called out for "a man down" in the street from an epileptic seizure or some other emergency to be attended to until the ambulance came.

One memorable day I was seeing patients when we heard a loud crashing sound coming from the road. I grabbed my small portable oxygen tank and my black doctor's bag and ran out into the street. There, right in front of the office, was an overturned car with wheels still spinning, spewing puffs of black smoke. Inside the upside-down vehicle was a single unconscious occupant, an elderly man. Without thinking or hesitating I opened the driver's side door, reached in and took the old man out of the stricken vehicle. I dragged him away to a safe distance and we all waited nervously. Fortunate-ly, the car didn't explode. Soon the ambulance arrived, stabilized the unconscious man and headed for the hospital with sirens blaring.

"That was close," I thought.

The next morning, I stopped into the man's room at the hospital after I was finished rounding on my patients.

"I'm the guy who pulled you out of your smoking car yesterday," I said with some pride.

"No you're not neither," said the ornery cuss. "I was coming to your office to get my records to send out to a new doctor when that damned accident happened."

This was less gratitude than I had expected, but then again I hadn't been killed lugging the old ungrateful bastard to safety. That was thanks enough I suppose.

There were so many appreciative folks that it made all the extra effort seem worthwhile. I often felt like a member of their extended families That was truly a great reward and a privilege to be cherished..

One of my favorite people was an elderly German fellow named Harry.

CHAPTER 32

Broadway Harry

I HAD BEEN HARRY Schneller's doctor for years. Once he was a tall handsome fellow with flashing bright blue eyes, thick wavy blond hair and a killer smile. That's what his wife Lo would tell me. Lo was short for Charlotte.

She said, "Every time he would walk into a room, all the girls would stop talking and look at him. That's why I always called him Broadway Harry."

She told me this story on several occasions in exactly the same words spoken in her thick but endearing German accent. She had married Harry over 50 years ago and they had grown old together. She was a tender-hearted stout woman in her 80's with a rather deep raspy voice. If you closed your eyes and listened to her, you could imagine that a tugboat captain was talking to you. But her lovely, long-suffering spirit always came through loud and clear. She had once been a beauty. Time had not been as kind to her as it had been to Harry. Her squarish face and wrinkled skin framed her smallish eyes, the left eyelid even lower than the right. The scattered age spots and deeply furrowed brow testified to the length of her days.

But what a wonderful character she was. She brightened my day whenever she came in and she always accompanied Harry for his check-ups. She would listen intently to Harry as he went on about this subject or that, then suddenly she would interject:

"Dats it Harry, dat.. is.. *it*!"

They had an old Ford pickup truck that he had painted red, white and blue and he had named it America. She had followed Harry on his adventurous life, even on a stint in Alaska. Now they were living in the Ship Ashore trailer park nearby. I looked forward to seeing them both coming in for a visit. I always knew I was in for an entertaining earful.

On one such occasion, as I was auscultating the back of his lungs with my stethoscope, I noticed a four-inch scar above his left shoulder blade. It sat in a shallow depression where fat and muscle had been lost. The scar itself was so well healed that I had not noticed it before even though I had examined his chest many times in the past.

"Harry," I said, "what's the story on this scar?"

"You really want to know?" he asked in his musical German accent. "OK, sure, I'll tell you".

Now, I would say Harry was still strikingly handsome considering his 85 years. He was still a strong and trim man with a warm disposition. His hair was curly and gray but there was still a gleam in his bright blue eyes when he smiled. I imagined him as young Paul Newman handsome.

He brightened as he related his story....and this is the honest truth as Harry told it to me. I'll have to paraphrase often and I'll need to speak in my own voice. It wouldn't be fair to Harry to try to imitate his choice of words or his accent. But the core events and people are just as he told them to me.

This is how he began his saga:

You know my father was a very wealthy and powerful man from Hamburg. He ran a big shipping company that had been in our family for generations. His ancestors had come over to Germany from England in the late 1700's. I was the oldest son and of course the whole family expected me to someday carry on the family business. I was seventeen and full of piss and vinegar. I wanted to follow my own vision, my own dreams. The childhood domination of my spirit had been severe in the old Central European style. So, one night I decided to elope and I married myself. I left.

That was early February of 1914 and I made my way down to Amsterdam. My journey along the way was propelled by the events I encountered. These details are not important but let me say I reveled in my sense of freedom and the unbridled life of a vital young searcher. I had a modicum of money. I ate and slept simply, so my needs were not great.

My plan was to get out to sea and follow my destiny wherever it might lead. In this endeavor I had been successful, having scheduled a berth on a steamer headed out for San Francisco under a German flag. I had signed on as an ordinary seaman expecting to perform the duties of a deck hand.

So it was, that I had come to have a drink at a crowded bar along the canal that lined Amsterdam's red-light district. There was a pleasant if not rough looking bunch in the house that cold winter night. Everyone seemed to take comfort in the warmth and shelter of the place. Most of the patrons were either sea-going types or other working-class men.

The lighting was subdued and gave a muted golden glow. The humming of the various conversations melded into one undulating murmur and the air was faintly clouded with the silvery haze of tobacco smoke.

I sat nursing a drink at the end of the long dark wooden bar. It was a massive structure with a long brass rod to support your feet. An elegant marble countertop spanned its entire length and was complemented with a fine wood trim. It faced a huge mirror encased in a dark wooden backbar that was ornately carved in the old-fashioned Dutch style.

I admired the craftsmanship of the woodwork and I was eyeing their copious selection of liquors when I felt a tap on my right shoulder. I turned around and to my surprise there stood a tall, elegant older man in a black fur top hat. He wore a tie with a vest and jacket that was concealed beneath a proper black overcoat accented with expensive fur lapels. The heavy coat covered his grey wool pants down to his mid calves. He wore expensive cordovan leather shoes that still held a bit of the snow he had brought in from the street outside. He had a well-trimmed grey mustache that highlighted the face of a still handsome yet stern patrician with intense blue eyes that were set beneath his thick black eyebrows.

"Father," I said, lost for words. I gathered myself and somewhat timidly asked, "How did you find me?"

"I have my ways son," he said sternly. "I have come all this way to take you home, Heinrich."

I felt a gut-wrenching pull of gravity, for I had always obeyed him with the loyalty he commanded of others. But I would not be deterred from my plans. In truth, I had not shared with him the reasons for my departure. I had felt that he would be incapable of sympathy for my yearning for freedom. How could I explain the realization that the trappings of wealth would never fulfill my desire for adventure, to forge my own identify,....how I harbored the dream of starting a new life in America?

I had not left a detailed note. It just said:

"My dear parents, please forgive my surprising you with such news. I am leaving home for a while and I promise to stay safe. I will write in time to let you know how things are going. Your loving son, Heinrich. "

Now I felt embarrassed and somehow ashamed.... yet I still remained determined.

"Father, I can't come with you. I am boarding a ship for San Francisco in the morning. I have signed onto the crew"

He said, "I have come this long way to bring you back home, son. If you do not come now, you will be considered lost to our family."

That was the last time I saw Father.

We set sail several days later and I watched Europe fade into my past from the deck of our steamer carrying freight bound for San Francisco. I thought about arriving in America and especially trying my luck in Alaska with its endless wilderness, natural bounty and its draw to the pioneer spirit.

Well, I won't trouble you with the details of the long sea voyage and the tedium of the life of a deck hand. I will pick up the story as we were passing the Pacific coast off Mexico near Mazatlán in August of 1914. The heat and humidity were oppressive on deck and I was attending my duties when the vessel lurched somewhat and then started to gradually slow to a crawl. There was quite a commotion on board and after some general confusion among the crew it became clear that the engines had failed and we had lost all power. We were forced to anchor within sight of the Mexican shore and were stranded for several days.

We were completely out of communication with the rest of the maritime world as the radio was not accessing contact. Attempts at repairing the damaged machinery failed. Finally, it was realized that it would be necessary to seek help on the shore if possible. I set out in a rowing launch with an officer and six other crewmen. We landed on the white sandy beach with lush palm covered hills behind them. It seemed at first blush that we had stumbled onto an idyllic haven. Soon we realized that there was a reception already in progress, for we had been closely observed since our anchorage.

A large group of horsemen, perhaps forty in number, appeared on the beach. In their large sombreros, white blouses and with chests crossed by bandoliers of bullets, the long mustachioed riders looked dangerous. Were these bandits? It was not clear, but there was the immediate pall of danger and it was obvious our reception committee was not pleased to see us.

"Who are you?" their leader growled in Spanish.

One of our number, who was fluent in their language explained.

"We are merchant seaman from that disabled German vessel that you see offshore. We had engine trouble and need help. We're dead in the water."

"Wait here." came the sharp retort. He and a number of their party took off at a gallop toward the tree line and the rest kept a close watch on our party with their rifles and pistols at the ready. We waited in the hot sun for several hours until finally more horsemen appeared. They were led by a different man with a threatening charismatic aura.

"How many men are on your ship?" he asked sharply from his saddle.

"We have 32 crewmen," was the answer.

"What do you carry and where are you headed?"

"We're bound for San Francisco with freight of various types"

"Bring your captain and all your crew ashore," he commanded brusquely, then he wheeled his horse around and headed back to the cover of the palms.

Over the next few hours, we ferried the captain and all the crew in packets to the shore until we were all gathered there. Toward sunset the chief reappeared with his minions on horseback. Guns were drawn and trained on each of us.

"Line up," he said.

Our captain protested but he was ignored.

"Line up I said!"

Sensing the hopelessness of resistance, we formed a line 33 men long.

"Where are you from *mi capitan*?"

The captain, Herr Gunter, spoke through the interpreter.

"We are a German vessel bound for San Francisco, we are not armed. Can you help us, our ship is without power?"

The Mexican chief surveyed the line of men coldly. "Are you all Germans?"

"No," said the captain. "We also have British, Dutch and American hands onboard."

"I want the Americans to stand together."

Captain Gunter was taken by surprise.

"What is the meaning of this?" he asked indignantly.

"Do it now!....stand them together!" was the angry retort.

....We looked at each other with uncertainty. What could this mean? Rifles and pistols began to waver a bit with fingers on triggers and reluctantly the eight Americans formed a group at the left end of the line. The leader of the horsemen raised his hand slowly and rifle shots rang out. The eight Americans fell dead on the sand.

"I am Poncho Villa, leader of these men, we hate Americans. You can join our army or you can join your American friends."

And so that is how I joined the Mexican fighters in their civil war.

We did not learn that Europe was engulfed in the flames of the Great War for quite some time. During the ensuing year I lost many of my comrades on the battlefield. We scrambled and fought to survive. There were many bloody engagements and in one pitched battle I was lying prone in a shallow trench when a rival Mexican fighter jumped on me and we violently tumbled about. In the scramble he stabbed me in the back with a long knife. I was able to kill him with my pistol but I was badly wounded. The knife blow must have penetrated my chest cavity because I coughed up some blood. And for weeks, I was short of breath with the smallest exertion. Anyway, that is how I got the scar you see here today.

It was necessary for me to recuperate for over a month and during that time we were encamped at Puerto Vallarta on the Pacific coast.... it lies somewhat south of Mazatlán. One day I saw a freighter flying the British flag lying at anchor out in the harbor.

This was my chance.

I waited until dark and then stealthily I stole to the shore and swam out to the ship, climbed up a line to the deck and hid in an obscure corner under some rigging. Within an hour a boat arrived from shore with a heavily armed party of Villa's men bearing torches. They boarded the ship and approached the captain.

Captain Jones was a born seafarer from London. He stood upright, always well-groomed with an affable personality but always in strict control of his crew and ship. This was his twentieth year in command and he had seen a lot in that time. This was different.

"Where is our man?" the leader of the boarding party rudely demanded.

Captain Jones responded through an interpreter, "To which man do you refer?"

"One of our men has gone missing and we think he's hiding on your ship."

"I know of no such man," said Captain Jones

"I have orders to search your vessel," the Mexican said with a sardonic smile that glinted with the flash of a golden front tooth.

"We are in your waters it is true," said the captain bravely, "I do object strenuously, but I can't stop you. We are unarmed. But we have nothing to hide. Look for yourself then."

And so, the members of the boarding party spread out throughout the ship in an hour-long search that did not turn up a stowaway. My heart raced as they tore randomly at crates, lifeboats and any hiding place they could imagine. But they somehow missed me. Grudgingly the suspicious group reentered their small craft and rowed back to the shore empty handed. Certainly, the camp would continue their search into the surrounding jungle throughout the night.

When an hour had passed and no other boats had appeared on the water, the captain called out in a loud voice,

"Alright you, come down now....Yes, you hiding up there, I want you to come down now."

I was at first stunned and I remained frozen in my hiding place. Did he really know I was there? How and when did he figure that out? To this day I don't know.

"Come on down now, I know you're up there," the captain repeated in a stern voice that had the ring of affection like a call to a pet or a child that would not come when summoned.

So, slowly I climbed down from my perch, and standing before him, my face was a mask of trepidation and anticipation. I looked him in the eyes. I was filthy, very thin, unshaven, and wearing worn-out pants and a ripped white shirt. I really was not looking my best. Here I was, running away from Poncho Villa into the arms of the British, a nation at war with my native homeland. What could I expect? My life was in the hands of this man that I had never met. I endured the painful seconds and then he asked:

"What is your name young man?"

"Harry Schneller, sir."

"Well then Schneller, are you familiar with the work aboard ship?"

"Yes Captain, I am a seasoned deck hand, sir."

"Good," he said, "we can always use a good deck hand. Now go down below, clean yourself up and get something to eat.... then find yourself a bunk."

At dawn we sailed away headed for California. And that, Doctor, is how I came to America with this scar on my back."

CHAPTER 33

One Night In The ER

I WAS ON CALL for unassigned patients that night. I was relaxed and nothing challenging had come in so far. In fact, it was quieter than usual. But when you wear the mantle of an ER doctor you must be prepared for anything. Soon I would be faced with a situation whose memory has lasted vividly these long years. The ambulance called us to prepare for a dire arrival. An eighteen-year-old was coming in with a chest wound from a 357 magnum pistol. He was conscious and his vital signs were stable.

My immediate reaction was to call in the surgeon and he appeared within minutes, calm and collected as always. I greatly admired the great skill and judgement he consistently displayed and it gave me an instant sense of relief that he would be there to manage what I feared might be a catastrophe. He had served a tour as an army surgeon in Viet Nam. He was no stranger to gunshot wounds and I relaxed a bit knowing he would lead and I would assist.

And so we waited with a composed sense of anticipation preparing the supplies and gathering the nurses, the respiratory technician and lab staff we would inevitably need. The blood bank was put on alert, for we would surely be tested with our limited inventory. The boy was being transferred from Brookings Oregon some thirty miles north of our town of Crescent City. The story would emerge later about the circumstances of his shooting. He had been down in the Brookings harbor with some friends hanging out and having fun.

Apparently, another carload of boys showed up and there was bad blood between the groups. He approached the car and kicked the door. One shot rang out and the young man dropped to the ground as the car took off.

Now Brookings is not a violent place, far from it. It is sleepy, prosperous and cleanly. It would be a nice town in which to retire with its stately shoreline homes. That this sorrow was approaching our ER from that direction was in itself a shocking surprise.

Soon we heard the sirens and I could see the flash of the red and orange lights in the receiving bay. I rushed out to greet the paramedics. They were wheeling in the gurney with two IVs of normal saline running full open, one in each arm. And then something strange happened. A handsome young man lay calmly on the gurney. He looked at me with a smile and said "Hi". His curly blond hair and clean-cut looks took me by surprise. His preppy dress and demeanor were not at all what I had expected. The encounter seemed more like the greeting from my waiter on summer break who was working at a fancy restaurant. His color was good, though there were a few beads of sweat on his brow.

We got him into the trauma room quickly and removed his clothes. He was smiling and passing pleasantries while we worked, his bright perfect teeth freely displayed. I saw the dime sized wound just below his right collar bone and my stethoscope revealed markedly reduced breath sounds on the right. There was a dull thud on tapping the chest wall with my hand on that side compared to the bright sounds on the left. The chest X ray confirmed the large quantity of blood that was accumulating on the right. His blood oxygen was starting to fall and he began to hyperventilate somewhat. His heart rate was accelerating. There was no time for a specific blood match. We had two lines of Type O negative blood, the universal donor type with the lowest chance of transfusion reaction, running full open with pressure applied by blood pressure cuffs around the infusion packets.

The surgeon quickly inserted a chest tube on the right and a profusion of bright red blood began to fill the vacuum bottle. His blood pressure was maintaining an adequate level and his breathing eased as we administered oxygen by nasal cannula. All the while he watched us work with a calm demeanor that conveyed confidence in our competence. He did not complain of pain or cry out. Not once.

As the surgeon and I entered the elevator on our way to wash up and prepare for the surgery he turned to me and tersely said " He's gonna die".

I was shocked. I was expecting him to be saved. He was talking to us. He seemed relaxed. Didn't we have things under control? Hadn't we gotten to him soon enough to stop the bleeding and send him home in a week or so? But the surgeon knew how such things went and the limits of the resources in our small rural county hospital. His battlefield experience had shown him what could and could not be done. We said no more as we scrubbed in and changed into shoe covers, surgical gowns, masks and gloves.

When we entered the OR he was already intubated and unconscious. The nurse anesthetist was administering oxygen with an ambu bag. As we approached his side taking our places and getting ready to open his chest, his pulse rapidly faded and then ceased. It all happened so fast. Though a hardened veteran of scenes of death, I was shocked. It was indeed hopeless. We could not resuscitate him despite our desperate efforts. He was young and virile and bright and now he was dead.

I relate this story to you some 35 years after it occurred but I can see it clearly now as I saw in then. Some scenes never leave you. It was with sorrow that I heard of the outcome of the shooter's trial. He was acquitted on the grounds of self-defense. I ask you how such a promising young man could be justifiably gunned down for kicking a car. I saw this boy and would have been proud to call him my son. I felt wounded when I heard of the verdict. True I was not at the trial and did not hear the testimony but It seemed inconceivable to me that he had been a mortal threat to anyone

Justice was not done that day.

CHAPTER 34

The Golden Age

THERE WAS A GOLDEN age of medicine in my lifetime but I only got to see its waning. The mighty buffalo herds, the blacksmiths and the barrel makers had all been eclipsed long before my generation but the doctor-patient relationship was still state of the art when I first began. It was a sacred and guarded place where no intrusions were allowed. The only consideration was the health of the human beings who had entrusted their welfare into your capable and compassionate hands. There was no computer in the room.

The doctor made and maintained eye contact. He or she spent their time talking, listening, examining, thinking, diagnosing, treating and teaching. And, after all that process, making sure that their instructions were well understood and that all issues were properly addressed. They performed thorough physical exams and took detailed histories.

I and many of my colleagues struggled to keep inviolate this place of privacy in every way we could but in the end the computer entered every room. Not because it is essential to provide excellent medical care. It brought the government and the insurance company into the equation.

There are obvious advantages to this shift. It potentially allows detection and avoidance of suboptimal care and it is intended to provide a handle on costs to name just a few. But the time and energy needed to navigate and produce the required documentation seriously interrupts the interaction with the patient. This creates a real threat to quality care.

It is simple math, the more time with the computer, the less time you have with the person before you.

To the doctors of the future, I say you must resist the tyranny of the chart. You must remember it is the human being you are treating, not the record.

I believe it is fundamental that we realize the importance of finding ways to have technology adapt to us rather that requiring us to adapt to it. Otherwise we may drown in the sheer volume of tasks required to process it. Technology should enable creativity, not hobble it.

CHAPTER 35

The Black Bag

THE LIFE OF THE rural General Practitioner is an iconic role. There is an element of the frontiersman in the spirit that drives him or her. They are heir to a long tradition, a remnant of the past when such independent and intrepid souls hung up their shingles in the wilderness and brought the science of the day to isolated outposts and towns.

In those days, they ministered to their patients as they lay in their own sick beds, not in a clinic or an impersonal hospital ER where such private moments occur these days. They shared the destiny of their communities, enjoying the beauty and serenity of the un-cluttered environment around them. They were not just another name you picked from a list. This local doctor was *the* person who showed up at your front door knocking. They were the person with the black bag who entered your home, sometimes at a moment of extreme crisis and vulnerability. They were, in a way, the very face of medicine, part scientist and part shaman, a vessel of hope.

When the doctor makes a house call today there remains a trace of this mystique, even in our connected electronic world. There lingers a vague reminiscence of this frontier isolation. It is especially true in the more rural villages and homesteads.

Entering a patient's home can seem like boarding a sailing ship that is confronting a storm. Uncertainty and danger may be imminent, actions may need to be taken and choices may need to be made; at times, life and death choices. What is appropriate in the home may differ from the considerations taken under the bright lights of a hospital ward.

No, here on the fringes, there is an unspoken sense that the affairs transpiring under this roof are unique and private. Factors, sometimes unforeseen, may emerge to take precedence within these rooms where for years family life has unfolded.

I want to relate a story to you about Doctor Thomas and a troubling situation that he encountered. The setting was a home visit, where the hot spotlight of outside observers vanished and high technology was not required, just a stethoscope, a prescription pad and his character.

HE CARRIED A BLACK bag. The one he bought the week before he started medical school. The first object that he had purchased as he paused to pass the threshold of a life's dream. It was just like the doctor's bag in the classic Depression era black and white photo. The doctor from the Midwest, tired, grim and determined, leaving his old Ford truck and about to enter through the screen door of a humble house where someone was sick and suffering, someone was crying out for relief. This was such a home and he clutched his bag and summoned the spirit that drove him to this place, this tiny town on a stretch of paradise.

Here were beautiful rolling green meadows and colorful lily bulb fields that lay buffeted between the giant redwood studded hills of verdant glory where the blue green luster of the pure Rogue River embraced the sea. He had come to this modest home, with its porch that faced the old schoolhouse, in response to a phone call from a family he had never met. They were in trouble and needed a doctor.

And so he knocked on the door, unaware of how dire the situation was that he was about to encounter.

"Hello doctor, I'm so glad you came, please come in," she said. "My husband is just inside in the living room."

Mary was sweet, middle aged, thin and plain to look at but clearly focused in her devotion and concern for her ailing husband who sat on the couch.

"Hello Jim," said Doctor Thomas, "I hear your leg is really in bad shape."

Jim flashed a weak smile and waved his hand in greeting.

"Doc," he said, "I'm not going to the hospital. I'd rather die, but I can't take this pain."

"Well, let's take a look," said the doctor.

Jim was a type 1 diabetic since age 18 and a heavy smoker. His right leg had been amputated above the knee a few years ago but now the trouble lay on the left. As he lifted his pant leg, Dr Thomas could smell the foul pungent odor of advanced infection and he saw the large gaping ulcer surrounded by hot red flesh that was consuming his shin. Slipping off the slipper from his blueish foot, the blackened toes confirmed that gangrene had set in. This leg must be sacrificed if he had any hope of survival.

"Jim this is bad, we need to send you to the hospital now for surgery and antibiotics."

"No," he said, "I lost one leg to diabetes and I'm not gonna' be a no-legged cripple sittin' on the porch watchin' the traffic go by."

The doctor looked up at his wife and he realized that a grim determination had seized this household. She was clearly resolved and Jim was far down the road to his fate. Yes, the healer had been called for help but only as an observer, a facilitator. This was not going to be a rescue.

"How old are you?" the doctor asked.

"Forty-eight," he said with a hint of defiance.

Just then his son, John, walked into the room and said hello. He appeared to be about twenty-five, a slim, small framed young man with soft almost fragile features. He stood resolutely next to his mother. Doctor Thomas could feel their unspoken question boring into him : "Will you help?"

"I don't know what to say. We can save your life if we act quickly. We should save your life. I know you're depressed, who wouldn't be, but you're young. Think of your family Jim, they love you, it's obvious."

Jim shook with a chill, clearly feverish. Beads of sweat formed on his brow and his pain was palpable as he squirmed a bit into the couch.

"Can you help me with the pain Doc, it's awful bad?"

The doctor paused, pondering the situation, but then focusing on his patient's immediate concern said, "Yes, I can help."

How could he not. He could provide comfort, but he knew he was not in control of the situation. Events were beginning to carry them all away as surely as that blue green river flowing to the sea.

He opened his bag and drew up a syringe of morphine. The injection took effect quickly and Jim relaxed a bit. They all took a moment to breathe.

The doctor sat down in a chair across the room. The home was tidy, the room painted in beige and brown. Simple but functional old wooden furniture was carefully arranged. Traces of the smell of breakfast still hung in the air and the warmth from the wood stove closed in a bit.

What now? What now?

The doctor took out his pad and wrote a prescription for liquid morphine.

"Here," he said handing the prescription to Jim, "this will buy you some time, but my very strong advice is to go to the hospital immediately. Will you at least take antibiotics?"

"No way!" Jim said with dead certitude.

With that, the doctor gathered up his things and with an empathetic gaze he wished patient, wife and son a sorrowful goodbye.

"I'll be back in the morning, please call me if you need anything before then. If you change your mind about getting proper treatment I'll admit you directly to the hospital."

Doctor Thomas closed the screen door behind him and as he stepped outside he grappled with what had just occurred. The moral, ethical and legal questions swirled through his mind. What should be done? What could be done? He knew that many would refuse to get involved. There were personal and professional risks in caring for such a patient. He was being asked to provide what could easily be called suboptimal care. Yet the need for timely compassion seemed paramount. His feet found the truck and after a short ride north on the coastal highway he was back in the fold of his family and home.

The next morning he knocked on their door not knowing what he would find. There had been no phone call during the night. Mary opened the door. She was tense. A jumble of fear, sorrow, confusion and determination seemed to have gripped her. The doctor sensed that it had been a long, hard night, as if daylight was breaking on a battlefield. He braced himself and summoned the solemnity suitable for this strange and pitiful moment.

She led him into a side porch that had been enclosed to form a long narrow bedroom. Jim was lying on a bed. He was ashen, racked with torment and perspiration but he was clear minded. He turned his head toward the doctor,

"Hello Doc."

"Morning Jim, you're not looking too good."

"I ain't too good."

He laughed faintly and his weak smile was uplifting to us all.

"You know it's still not too late to turn this thing around, we can call an ambulance." .

"I ain't goin' nowhere." he glared defiantly.

He settled down a bit and took a deep breath. Regaining his composure he asked softly, "How much of this morphine would it take to kill me?"

The doctor was taken aback by this logical question, one that should never be asked but now seemed unavoidable.

"There's a lot of medicine in that bottle but you should take it as it says on the label."

Their son John walked in and stood next to the bed. He put his hand on his father's chest and Jim grasped it tenderly. It was then that I saw the first tears welling up in Mary's eyes.

"He begged me last night to shoot him but I just couldn't do it," she said.

Doctor Thomas looked at her earnestly, "You must promise me you won't do that. After this is all over, you'll still be alive and you'll have to answer for it like a criminal. People may not be able to understand why you did it, they may not let it go.'

He turned to Jim and said,

"Don't let them do it. If it has to be that way, you need to pull the trigger yourself." Somehow the doctor knew Jim couldn't do it. He lay there quietly and looked away.

There are times when logic deserts us and the wind drives our sails. Dr Thomas was not in control of this foundering ship and exactly where it was sailing was unclear, yet everyone knew it was headed for the rocks without a pilot.

There was little more to do or to say. The good doctor said his goodbyes to the embattled family. Their eyes embraced with sorrow.

"God bless you and guide you," he said as he stepped out into the morning sunshine and rejoined the living world.

That was the last time he saw or spoke with any of them. Jim died sometime that night without any signs of violence. He was buried, after a wake, in the nearby church cemetery. Doctor Thomas heard of no inquest or inquiry. He was glad of that. It was better that way.

CHAPTER 36

Moving South

AFTER 12 YEARS OF rural solo practice it was time to reevaluate. By then we had three employees and Lisa was able to stay at home with our two beautiful young daughters. We had long since moved into our modest but comfortable first home ensconced in the lushness of long-ago logged forest land. The giant redwood stumps arrayed around our little acre stood as testimony to that bygone era. It was with sorrow, yet a great sense of relief, that I began to look for another path.

Times had changed. A maximum-security prison was built in the middle of our redwood paradise. The ever-present lights had destroyed the brilliance of the nighttime sky in the fading wilderness we had come to love.

Fading wilderness...that seemed to be emblematic of my professional world as well.

Unfortunately, time was running out on the viability of my business model. The insurance companies and the government had intruded more and more until even my modest financial goals became untenable. I was forced to give up private practice and my vaunted independence. Eventually I would chose to become employed by people who could handle the business issues. This freed me up so that I could concentrate my energies on the care of the sick. Still, I would not have traded those 12 years for anything.

It took courage and maybe a bit of naivete to hang up a shingle in the middle of nowhere and go it alone for as long as I did. But I was able to use the full skill set I had acquired with such hard work in residency and I got to be my own boss. I had inherited that inclination from my beloved father and it was something I cherished. Sadly, the burdens imposed eventually proved to be too high a price to pay, even for a stubborn old bastard such as myself.

I found a recruiter and soon I hooked up an interview in Ventura, California. Within four months I became a member of a Health Maintenance Organization down there, what people call an HMO, a practice that provided full coverage to its patients for a monthly premium.

I felt as if I had entered into the belly of the beast. We were a group of over fifty doctors in a somewhat urban setting. It took a while to adjust from the independence of solo practice but it did have many advantages and Ventura is a very lovely town in which to spread your wings.

The organization had been serving the community for many decades before I arrived. It had a good reputation and a great medical staff. This HMO was dedicated to providing the best and most comprehensive services for the lowest possible price. I would receive a salary, far better than I had been paying myself, and finally I would be free of the burdens of running a small business and having to collect fees directly from patients.

This concept seemed to align well with my wish to remove factors such as reimbursement from distorting the doctor-patient relationship. No matter how value based my services may have been in private practice, there was the reality of staying afloat financially and therefore the need to collect fees directly from the folks I treated. I found this a distraction not an opportunity and my new working arrangement did dispense with much of that tension.

But at an HMO, other issues would arise such as getting costly services or tests approved through the process of committee decision making. This was a different kind of interference. I had not previously needed a second opinion as to whether a test I considered necessary could be performed.

After a while I began to view such a committee function as being a new opportunity for patient advocacy and I was not shy in expressing my opinion that concerns for the patient should always come first. Finding the right balance between thoroughness and economy proved to be a difficult task at times but my group was very diligent and I was proud to be part of their effort.

In the long run, I would spend many more years trying to unhitch dollars from the services I rendered. It would later drive me into government medicine, first at the Veterans Administration and then the Armed Forces. But there was no panacea for the intrusions into the relationship of doctor and patient wherever you looked.

In my later years in government service I encountered restricted drug formularies, testing restrictions and limited specialty referral choices. There was no escaping the future and the future was focused on reducing payor costs no matter what format of health care delivery you might want to choose. The best I found I could do was to adapt and try to minimize the obstacles in my way and maintain focus on fashioning together the most favorable circumstances for the people I served. I know they appreciated this. The concern and effort bonded patient and doctor in the quest to relieve their physical and emotional burdens. One way or another, needs were met.

I knew that my patients did not want to think their physician had conflicts of interest. They relied on me to access the best choices possible for their care. They also worried that the exorbitant costs of care might lead to financial hardship or even family ruin. To me this was at the heart of the commitment to my life's work. I was their advocate, their navigator through a system that they could not possibly traverse adequately alone.

"Do unto others as you would have them do unto you" says the golden rule. It required a lot of extra time and effort to tailor care in that way. I am proud to say that this commitment never wavered. Like Gary Cooper in *High Noon,* I always tried to hang up my guns as I walked out of town with my head held high.

CHAPTER 37

Ventura California

MOVING TO VENTURA COUNTY was also a breath of fresh air from a lifestyle point of view. Thus began a wonderful transformation in the life of our family. We bought a small ranch in a beautiful canyon just east of the town of Ventura, in the wild hills of a remote corner of Santa Paula, California. This was a time in life when our little nuclear unit bloomed. Lisa, Viena, Bailey and me. We all still share the joyful memories that formed there.

Even though we were blessed with all the gifts in life that any reasonable person might desire, I was still racked with a strange sense of existential isolation that became particularly intense during this period. It seemed an odd irony since my life was so full. In many ways this was the highpoint of our family life.

I wrote a lot of poetry during this period and I would occasionally venture downtown to Cafe Voltaire on open mic night and try out new material. At best, it would earn a smattering of polite applause. I felt that I was debuting great new works of literature, not so much thought the audience. I knew they were not prepared for the depth of the material. I must admit it hurt my feelings a bit when my eight-year-old daughter got a rousing ovation for her original offerings. Such are the slings and arrows of outrageous fortune.

I do have to admit that she was damned cute and precocious.

Though I had a plethora of human contact in my life, I still felt a profound and strange loneliness, a disconnection that I found difficult to escape or even understand.

CHAPTER 38

The Professor of Literature

MANY YEARS LATER I had the pleasure of meeting a most intelligent and sensitive soul with whom I could discuss such matters. He seemed a disembodied spirit, at least to me. We had only communicated by email. I am sure he was a living breathing man but we never met in the flesh. Regardless, he was very kind and read my poetry and prose. He gave me encouragement which I very much appreciated and he offered advice from time to time.

He was older than me and had long held the Chair of English Literature at a prestigious university. It was so encouraging to be able to share our common interest in literature and philosophy.

He was considering retirement when we met. Looking back on his life, he said he had been in exile. It was a self-imposed exile to be sure and he said that he enjoyed life that way. I think what he meant by exile was that he had felt a welcome detachment from the everyday world of commerce and things. He had found solace and refuge in a world of ideas and he had flourished within the haven of his academic community.

He had said that he thought I had also chosen a life of exile.

This was insightful, but not quite correct, for I had not chosen my existential distance. I had come to feel a strange and profound sense of spiritual isolation that I struggled to understand and somehow escape.

Those beautiful years in Ventura had been burdened with this struggle. I had had plenty of contact with loved ones and patients, yet I still perceived a disabling and perplexing sense of alienation. I would wander about seeking something I couldn't quite identify clearly and I sought out unknown souls to discuss it with. It was a debilitating loneliness in a sea of contact and I found it bewildering.

I began to write poetry with much more urgency and volume. It seemed to be a tonic and provided an arena where I could sort out these baffling forces that I felt impinging upon me.

This led to profound spiritual development and the exploration of the relationship between my existence and the rest of creation. For we are inextricably connected to all around us yet paradoxically confined to the sphere we know as ourselves. Breaching this paradox and accepting it rather than feeling confined by it helped me to overcome that strange feeling of estrangement.

I found that in the course of developing my own poetic voice and style, philosophical and artistic impulses were melded and thought permeated emotion in a way that was different from other authors I was reading.

I was not enjoying most of the modern popular poetry I encountered. It seemed too heavily steeped in personal emotion without advancing profound ideas of compelling cognitive and spiritual power. As I saw it, there was a danger that popular verse might become relegated to song lyrics, greeting cards and to the rapid, short and angry rhymes of rap or the displays of raw emotion and frustration expressed at poetry slams.

It seemed to me that "serious" poetry was becoming a pursuit for elitists. There was too much idiosyncratic language and abstract imagery. It didn't seem to move me, nor was there a clear message being conveyed. Themes seemed content to lie between the lines where scholars could speculate on its meaning.

I was disappointed to find that I seemed to have had more in common with poets who were long dead and at risk of being forgotten. Worse, I found few contemporaries who enjoyed reading or hearing my efforts.

That type of rejection is a particularly frustrating. You must struggle to maintain confidence in the power of your heartfelt work. The public is often inattentive to new forms of expression until its value is widely recognized. I am reminded of Vincent Van Gogh who sold only one painting in his lifetime, to his beloved brother Theo. Fortunately, I still have both my ears.

God bless poor Vincent, you tortured soul.

So I attempted to write probing verse and prose that would be comprehensible and moving to the many. I felt as if I was fulfilling a special need in a world bombarded by sheer entertainment. I was driven by the hope that if I found it moving, others might also. The achievement of such a feat separates the acclaimed from the lonely garret artist. Playing that out on the stage of life is the only real proving ground.

CHAPTER 39

What Lurks Below,
(Circa 1990)

I ADMIRE THE SOCRATIC search for virtue and the striving for integrity to guide our conduct. Such choices are at the crux of the character we manifest. The potential for great good and great evil are inherent in all of us and to nurture one pole of this dichotomy often requires the concealment of the other.

Wartime is the classic mirror that reflects the necessity to abandon the qualms and the equivocations of a high-minded morality. Primitive imperatives require primitive and brutal actions.

In normal times, circumstances don't require us to confront such unpleasant realities. But even in tranquil well-ordered lives there can manifest situations wherein this disparity is revealed for what it is. The unmasking of the face of evil within us in times of peace and plenty can come as a surprising and unwelcome shock. When that which is hidden is exposed, when light unexpectedly illuminates the darker foundations of our moral edifice, the howling of the Furies can sometimes be heard.

At such an incongruous moment, when serenity would normally prevail, anomalies may come into focus that can baffle and deeply unsettle us. Suddenly the reflected being that we now see seems foreign to our well-manicured self-image, foreign yet instantly recognizable. At such a moment, a flood of guilt, of shame or buried bitter memories may reemerge. Images appear that must be tamped back down to allow the spirit to regain its footing in the realm of the groomed life, the life one has so diligently crafted to fit into a world of functionality. The lid must be slammed down, the door shut tight and normality must be restored.

Such a flashing reckoning, a brief immersion into a perspective one can pass through but dare not inhabit, such a situation is the subject of the story I now present.

THE DOWNPOUR WAS TORRENTIAL. The kind of a night when sheets of rain blind you and you want to pull over if only it were safe but the traffic just won't let you. He decided not to try it. He had come to Laguna Beach to buy the large oil painting he so loved. It was called the Gardener's Daughter and was a beautiful impressionistic portrait of a young woman in a long colorful floral dress. She had thick honey-colored hair that cascaded onto her shoulders and she was seated sweetly in a chair. There was a still life of a basket of fruit and a vase filled with flowers on a small table next to her. The big floppy hat framing her lovely hair and face was sensational. It seemed to capture the essence and the loveliness of his young wife. He was on a mission to surprise her with this gift for their new home.

They had two wonderful young daughters and had just purchased a small ranch in a canyon outside of Ventura California. Star filled nights graced the hillsides that surrounded them and creatures abounded with no purpose other than to roam about happily. Pigs, cats, dogs, sheep, horses, parrots, peacocks, chickens and roosters thrived without care while the coyotes and mountain lions contemplated their options outside the fence.

He was a family doctor with a rewarding practice and a good reputation. Things were going well.

But tonight, the rain would not let up, so he drove over to the nearby Laguna Hotel and checked into that storied lodging where the stars of Hollywood's bygone heyday had once idled away their weekends. He was expecting to find a faded gem from another era but the years had not been kind to the old icon.

The halls seemed somewhat dingy, dark and narrow. He put the long black metal key into the lock and opened the door to a small and rather drab room with no special appointments. A faint odor of mustiness permeated the air. At least it was a dry place to spend the night and he was grateful just for that.

Weary, he sat down on the bed and looked into the mirror that hung above the small dresser in front of him. He was surprised by his reflection for he saw a tired and beaten man staring back at him. It was as if he was looking at a stranger. He could find no reason to explain what happened next. His face seemed to distort. Scars and open wounds began to appear while flashes of repressed painful memories emerged in rapid succession as if a growling dangerous force was trying to escape from within him. He suddenly felt totally exposed, he was not in control, he had to look away.

When he looked back, the vision had vanished. He sat there awhile, shaken and confused. His heart pounded a bit and then it settled down.

"What the hell was that?" he wondered.

"What triggered that bullshit?"

Maybe it was the odd atmosphere and unexpected shabbiness of the hotel, maybe just fatigue. He tried to make sense of it, but a deep sleep overtook him.

In the morning he awoke to a lovely Laguna Beach day. Life was again as it should be. He found his blue Volvo station wagon parked on the street in front of the hotel where he had left it the night before. The oil painting lay securely inside, concealed under a blanket. It was a relief to find both car and art undisturbed.

He started the engine and pulled the car out into the slow parade of traffic heading north on the Pacific Coast Highway which, on that stretch, also served as Main Street. He passed the carved wooden likeness of the Greeter, a legendary gent who would wave to motorists passing south from that corner many decades ago.

A little further down the street he passed the giant wall painting of Wyland's whales and then the art gallery where he had purchased the painting. At the next corner he turned right onto Laguna Canyon Road and soon passed the large art exhibition grounds on the left with its ticket booths and the multiple entry gates that faced the road.

He recalled many a visit there to enjoy the extensive art shows. They had always featured high quality work by locals who resided in and around this legendary artist colony.

The events of the previous evening had left a vague sense of uneasiness that was hard to define, but as he drove past familiar surroundings, the tension started to unwind. It was always hard to leave Laguna Beach, there were so many happy memories for the family in this beautiful town by the sea.

A few miles up the canyon road, on the right, was the site of the Pageant of the Masters. Here, incredible illusions were created in the amphitheater under the night sky.

Onto the stage a huge picture frame was hauled and behind it was placed an elaborate set. Then actors appeared in intricate costumes and makeup, climbing into place, taking their positions on the set. Finally a painted backdrop was placed behind all of this to complete the scene.

The house lights would suddenly go dark and the thirty-piece orchestra would begin a dramatic musical introduction. The stage lights came back on and there before your very eyes was *The Last Supper* as if you were looking at Leonardo's original mural. Between the clever makeup, the lighting and the shadows, the actors no longer appeared to be living beings but rather integral parts of a painting. It was sheer visual magic. Jesus and the twelve apostles were sitting or standing in the exact positions and attitudes they had occupied in the great Renaissance masterpiece on that famous convent wall in Milan. Not a muscle moved on stage for ninety seconds while the narrator, in a beautiful baritone voice, described the work and the great significance of its contribution to the history of art. Then the lights went out and the illusion broke up into its constituent parts once again. Only the sounds onstage exposed its dismantling in the darkness.

Reminiscing, he cranked up the CD player, rolled down the windows and took in the fine Southern California morning. He leaned against the car door, settling back into the driver's seat with his elbow out the window, enjoying the crisp air whistling by. It had been wise to wait out that dangerous storm last night. Now he merged onto Highway 5 North, hit the accelerator and started to make good time.

He had hours to mull over the odd occurrence at the mirror the night before. Somehow, like a waking nightmare, the frightening vision had come and fled, its meaning a mystery. Why such thoughts, why now? It was as if something from the buried past had flashed its face, a beast with dangerous impulses that needed to be beaten down until they were no longer detectable. Out of the light and shadows of his imagination a startling psychic panorama had unexpectedly materialized and just as suddenly disappeared.

Life itself would have to reveal the significance, if any, of this strange event. Forget about this troubling anomaly, he thought. He was carrying home his cherished gift. It was such a splendid surprise, such a successful trip. The anticipation began to grow as he imagined his wife's joy upon seeing the painting. She had no idea that that had been the purpose of his mission south. He would drive the last five miles up the scenic and winding Wheeler Canyon Road with its light pink apricot groves in full bloom.

Passing the occasional horse ranch where Western movies were filmed years ago, the road shadowed the large stream that had formed this beautiful canyon. It was a stream that sometimes transformed itself into a raging river when the winter rains tore up the asphalt and prevented passage.

As the road ascended the foothills, the canyon walls pressed closer around both sides until it neared the top of the hill. There a small dirt road led off to the left. Through an automatic gate and past a few homesteads he would find the live oaks of his little ranch and the promise of sanctuary. Tomorrow he would head back to the clinic and to business as usual.

At that horizon
Where the eye beholds the soul
Narcissus kneels down at the water's edge
And reflects on the depths below
His image once proud is now pierced with wounds
They stare back at him
Gaping in a mask
Suddenly he is naked in the light of day
Without secrets
And he casts his eyes away

Slumped like words dissembled
Posing to amass some meaning
Yet sadly vainly drained of feeling
He draws the breath of self-estrangement

He has seen the face of his illusion
And he longs beneath the weight of sorrow
To set his listing soul aright
To hear a whisper break the silence
The echo of an ancient spirit
That would not dumbly let him drown
Would bid him lift his shaken visage
Would bid him hurry homeward bound

Sometimes it is the fleeting glimpse
Which is the most profound.

Painting of the Laguna Beach Hotel as seen from the beach

204

CHAPTER 40

Atheon

I HAD THE GREAT blessing of living on a small seven-acre ranch in a canyon just outside of Ventura California in the 1990's. Wheeler Canyon with its beautiful winding mountain road alongside its creek was lined with ranches, homesteads and blooming light-pink apricot orchards. It led to our little road, Live Oak.

There you entered a small offshoot canyon with its own little creek. At the end of the road, about a half mile, was said to be an old Indian burial ground. All around were hills that completely encircled you and at night the stars were brilliant and shining.

We watched the Hale-Bopp comet from head to tail as if it were a giant vehicle moving through the heavens with headlights. Our comfortable white stucco home with turquoise trim and orange Spanish tiled roof had beautiful double French doors all the way around. The portico with its red flooring had white pillars every 10 feet, each engulfed by red bougainvillea vines. The covered walkway completely surrounded the house. From the road it had the appearance of a Greek temple.

We named it Atheon.

Here for happy years my beautiful and loving family, Lisa, Viena, Bailey and I whiled away the hours in peace and harmony. Our pets seemed to multiply and soon we had three horses, five dogs, eight cats, three parrots, three sheep, two pigs, countless love birds, chickens, and peacocks. There was room and food for all and plenty of space to play.

The land swept steeply to a ridge top with purple, yellow and green fields lining the ascent. I would sit for hours and contemplate all this beauty under the warm and bright blue California sky. I would have been happy to spend my entire life working that land but various circumstances intervened and we decided that we should return to the East Coast.

As I looked out onto the hillside during our final days on the ranch, I was impressed by how stunning this beauty was. Yet I sensed that it was already fading into memory before my eyes. There is a special nostalgia at a moment like this; one of both appreciation and a feeling of loss. It is a sadness that is a blessing to behold. In this transient world it is our fate that all things must pass. George Harrison said that. On that we both agree.

FAREWELL TO WHEELER CANYON

Sand Creek where the memories run deep
And the bones of the Elders drink in ghosted shirts
Sand Creek where Wheeler Canyon speaks
With its muted tongue
Pressed against the leaves
Ever flowing toward the sea.

Here harm passed over us
Like an angel starbound in the brilliant night
Cast out above the halo of hills
That encircled us umbilically
Leaving us in peace
All in good California time

There is nostalgia of a certain kind
When that which is passing
Seems already gone
I miss it now as I did then
Never able to hold the golden wind, the flowers or the perfect sky

CHAPTER 41

Young Men and Chocolate

BEFORE WE LEFT FOR the East Coast, Lisa and I had a wonderful experience that I would like to share with you.

Beatrice Wood was an American artist best known for her works in pottery. She was also known as the Mama of Dada because of her close and romantic ties to key artists of that artistic movement in the early twentieth century. She was designated a National Treasure and maintained an active studio until her death at the age 105. She was famous for her appreciation of young men and her love of chocolate.

One fine bright southern California day my wife and I were driving the magnificent back country mountain road from Santa Paula to Ojai. We were past the sulfur springs and the Catholic seminary. The top was down, it was a balmy joyride. I was relaxed and in the moment.

Lisa said, "I met an interesting man at the store the other day. He was from India. He said he was Beatrice Wood's assistant and that maybe we would like to attend her birthday party. He gave me the address of her studio and it's on this road."

"That is interesting," I said, "that would be an honor."

So, we drove along the stretch of road sparsely dotted with horse ranches and homesteads that were set upon long green meadows. Eventually, we found the mailbox of the address she had been given. We wrote a note saying we had dropped by and that we wanted to go to the party, please phone us.

Somewhat to my surprise the phone call came.

One week later, on another beautiful and sunny March day, we were going up the crushed stone driveway leading to her home. It was a modest ranch house that also served as her studio. We entered through the open door and soon realized we had joined a ceremony of homage.

Beatrice was sitting on a small couch perched like a queen on a throne and many admirers were greeting her in a line while others were browsing the displays of her artwork arrayed around the room. Many Indian guests were there. The ladies wore beautiful and colorful Saris with head coverings. Their jewelry and facial make up adorned their smiling faces. The actress Rue McClanahan was there as were many others that I didn't recognize.

We had brought our six-year-old daughter Bailey with us. She sat on Beatrice's lap and they talked earnestly to each other. Bailey was an extremely bright and precocious child, so beautiful and bubbling with vivacious playful energy. With her long blond braids, I was sure she reminded Beatrice of her own young self. They spent some time together, both chatting away and she gave Bailey a little plum-colored bottle of her personal perfume. It had a subtle floral scent.

Though Beatrice was 104 years old that day, she was still beautiful. The remnants of her charismatic charms were obvious and she exuded an energy that was truly remarkable. She had long thick braided elegant gray hair wrapped into a bun and wore a long white dress. Her brilliant blue eyes conveyed warmth and humor. But the hypnotic communication of her glance is what surprised me the most.

The following poem was a contemporaneous attempt to capture the delightful event that was unfolding in the room.

YOUNG MEN AND CHOCOLATE
(In Memory of Beatrice Wood)

I saw her for the first time on her birthday
Her one hundred and fourth

She was greeting Indian friends dressed in their bright silk saris
Accepting gifts
While Love and Homage danced

Around the room her art was placed
Admired by those who adored her
Eyeing her playful treasures
Each with their own fond memories

But when I looked up and saw her radiant blue eyes
Longing eyes
That beckoned to me seductively
I stood stunned

Slowly she turned away
Toward my beautiful wife
Who offered a book
Of children
Dressed like vegetables in a garden
Like unspoiled fruit
And her ancient luminescent smile
Flashed out to embrace her with tender thankfulness
Perched on a small couch

Like a whimsical throne
Her elegant gray hair
Set beautifully against her white dress

ON THE RIDE HOME Lisa said to me, "Beatrice told me something very interesting. She said she gave Isadora Duncan that scarf that accidentally strangled her. She said it got caught in the wheel of the car she was riding in, the poor thing. That was so sad, I didn't know they were friends."

I had done a bit of reading before we set out that day.

"She and Isadora were both glamorous and shockingly liberated rebels in their day. They were friends and ran in the same circles " I said, "I bet they both left a trail of broken hearts."

CHAPTER 42

Life Is A Beach

WE HEADED BACK EAST and I got a job with the VA at an outpatient facility in Myrtle Beach, South Carolina. We spent 8 happy years living a block from the Atlantic shore. We had scaled back our menagerie to two dogs, four cats and three parrots with an occasional squirrel thrown in when storms orphaned the darling little tree climbing rodents.

I loved taking care of the Veterans at the clinic who were uniformly appreciative of good medical care and deserving of every bit that we could provide. The entire staff of the clinic worked so very hard to answer the complex needs of our Veterans. The bureaucracy of the VA management, however, was beyond intrusive into the day-to-day clinical matters. It seemed that new procedural guidelines were introduced every month. Apparently senior management, where protocols were formulated, were not aware that doctors prefer a stable work environment. Physicians naturally prefer to get things done in time tested ways that are peer reviewed and accepted voluntarily. It seemed to me that someone in an office somewhere was being paid a salary and it was their job to make changes. So, changes would be made, a lot of them and often.

They were going to tell me what those changes were without consulting me for my opinion. That is not a good way to treat scientific minds with independent spirits. Invariably the new guidelines were not helping me perform my work. In fact, usually it was an aggravating hindrance that added more and more diversions of my attention. The micromanagement became truly stifling. Even the thermostats were controlled by someone in Charleston, 100 miles away. The result was three different zones of temperature as you walked from the lobby to my office at the back end of the clinic. I rebelled, I protested.... but in the end, I felt compelled to move on. It became a health issue for me, both physical and mental.

I had been coming home late into the night, finishing documentation and performing tasks that would have been easy to delegate to my support team if management didn't insist that the MD do it themselves. These were functions I had delegated safely for decades to my staff until some genius upstairs decreed that the new VA methodology must be obeyed.

I became dangerously exhausted. I would not abandon my mission to be scrupulously thorough in caring for this very high-risk population. I would still take the time to listen and to probe. It was my goal not to let a single Veteran leave my office with an unattended important diagnosis or proper treatment. To do this, it was necessary for me to devote many hours after the clinic was closed to finish the day's documentation and attend to the myriad tasks required to provide comprehensive care for the 1200 complicated souls in my patient panel.

There were frequently long periods when loss of providers would occur. The turnover rate was very high due to the stressful conditions. This would then require the remaining staff to take on their workload. It might take 6 months or more to replace a vacancy.

After a few years, I was the provider with the longest tenure. I was a stubborn man and didn't quit until long after it had become intolerable.

In efforts to relieve my frustrations I bought an old 32-foot wreck of a cabin cruiser and rented a slip in a marina a bit further up north. Though this eventually ate my bank account alive, it introduced me to an enduring love of the element of water. I am very grateful for that part of my education. Boaters, boat dealers and particularly independent marine mechanics, tend to be a social type unto themselves. *Caveat Emptor*, buyer beware, but try to enjoy the ride. One unique personality from my seafaring days stands out in my mind.

CHAPTER 43

The Freckle King

You might say he looked classically Irish, whatever that might be, but he sure didn't look like a gypsy. Yet that was what I had heard others say about him. Some folks said he was descendent of the Irish Travelers. The Travelers had a long history of wandering across the Emerald Isle in stylized wagons, doing odd jobs, being feared for their reputation of thieving and bare-knuckle fighting.

He didn't look like a fighter either, more like a rough and tumble lover. He reminded me of a modern-day Falstaff. He was in his mid-sixties, tall and fair yet with a somewhat ruddy complexion and he had many fine freckles all over his face and body. His wavy blond-red hair was kept clipped to a moderate length atop a friendly round face with a ready smile. His blue eyes seemed to gleam a bit with a hearty welcome and he always seemed to be awaiting the next laugh.

Joe Haggerty was seriously obese with a large white and freckled protuberant abdomen without any folds of fat, like a huge rotund ball with a large belly button in the center. It gave him the look of a large sea mammal when he wore a bathing suit. He drank heavily and you just knew he had lived, and wanted to continue to live, as large as his dollars could muster. As much money as he could scrounge up would be a more accurate description of his means.

Though he was always broke, he managed to acquire an apartment, a house and a junkyard that he considered a used boat display case for patrons with active imaginations. Whether he ever sold a single vessel from his fleet of junk is anyone's guess. In the end it didn't matter. Some unknown detractor of his set the whole yard on fire one night and reduced the entire inventory to a pile of ashes. There were too many people who wanted Joe's hide to ever narrow down the list. The perpetrator was never uncovered.

Joe lived in his apartment at the marina on the intracoastal waterway. It lay at the northern edge of South Carolina where he docked his 60-foot double decked fishing boat. It had lower and upper cabins, a fish spotting tower at the top of a tall steel ladder and had a rotating radar unit. There was a panel full of instruments at the helm that sat behind the wide cabin window of the wood paneled pilot room. This ancient sailor of the sea, I am now referring to the boat and I'm putting it kindly, was a vintage vessel, his beloved Double D. I never asked Joe how the name came about but I had a theory. He loved women and Lord knows he always had an attentive older lady to look after his mundane affairs, and any pressing physical needs that might pop up.

Captain Haggerty, as he preferred to be called, was absolutely brimming with stories. We had met on S dock. We had adjoining moorings at the end of the long, floating catwalk and as I worked on my old 32-foot Wellcraft, I would admire the Double D and the parade of customers he would ferry out for a day of fun. He usually anchored off Bird Island. This was a beautiful place just before the intracoastal waterway joined the Atlantic.

We would shoot the shit and drink beer when we were both hanging out on our boats between his trips entertaining tourists. It looked like an inspired business model that he had concocted. His meter was running doing the very thing he loved best...piloting his beloved ship with packets of happy and skimpily clad young ladies carousing on the main deck, climbing stairs, sniffing around while they sipped cocktails, always excited by the smell of the salt air, the dancing dolphins and all the charms of the scenic beauty that was surrounding them.

Joe had grown up on the outskirts of Charlotte North Carolina. In those days the area was still quite rural. His Daddy and Momma ran a small country store and one day ten-year-old Joe was out back stacking up empty soda pop bottle returns. He looked up and realized he was penned in by a semicircle of roughneck teenagers. Not just any roughnecks, these were Lumbee Indians.

Now, the Lumbee were famous for their courage and independence. They had lived along the Cape Fear River long before history was recorded. During the Civil War, the Confederate Home Guard had tried to press their forefathers into forced labor for the construction of Fort Fisher near Wilmington. It was said that many men of the tribe had hid out in the swamps rather than accept that fate.

Well, young Joe was aware of their reputation and when he heard the click, click, click of switch blades he began to panic. Just then he heard the racking of a shotgun and his mother yelled out:

"You touch one little hair on my red headed baby and I'll blow ya 'all to Kingdom Come!"

Knives dropped to the ground in unison and the toughs disappeared. That was his Momma.

Now Joe had an amazing assortment of freckles and when he was about 8 years old Momma entered him in the State Freckle Contest. The competition was fierce, to hear him tell the tale, but he was ultimately crowned the new Freckle King. The honor was completely ruined when he was forced to kiss the Freckle Queen, a shy, embarrassed redheaded 8-year-old girl. Apparently, his taste for women had not yet manifested, but the nickname stuck with those who knew him way back when.

He had a lifelong romance with the sea and had been in the Navy when JFK ordered the blockade of Russian shipping headed for Cuba back in October of '62. He was onboard one of the ships of the line when they challenged and turned back a Russian vessel in the Caribbean. As he told it, he needed a change of underwear that day.

When he got out of the Navy, he started selling cars in Florida. He was a natural salesman of the master bullshitter variety. When he tired of that he decided to try his hand at pro wrestling. To be fair, Joe was sturdily built in those days and he really thought he might have a future at that game.

He made his debut in the Miami area. It didn't go well. First of all the crowd was small and the purse was even smaller. He took a run at the other guy in tights and before he knew what was happening, he was airborne and flying over the ropes. He landed on some metal folding chairs in the front row, bounced off and did a header onto the concrete floor. The next thing he remembered was coming to three days later in an ICU, intubated and surrounded by relatives.

A further career change was in order.

He was a hard man to kill. Years later, in his mid-sixties, he was working under his truck. He had it jacked up with a tire off. The jack slipped out and the truck came crashing down onto his lower chest and abdomen with full force. His horrified girlfriend saw the whole spectacle unfold before her eyes and had the presence of mind to jack the truck back up. Somehow, she managed to extract his 290-pound frame, loaded him into her car and drove the 15 minutes to the local ER. She didn't even think about calling an ambulance. Now that is one tough lady. She parked the car, ran inside and alerted the staff who promptly retrieved him on a stretcher. He was slipping fast.

Three days later I visited him in the ICU. His lady, angel that she was, sat faithfully beside him. Tubes were coming out of him from all sorts of angles and I have to say, the fact that he was still talking seemed nothing short of a miracle. As I was leaving, I leaned over and kissed him on the forehead. He looked up at me with that impish smile of his and said in a weak voice:

"When the world ends there will be cockroaches and Joe Haggerty."

He did have a point.

I hear he did well and got active again but I had to move my boat and we lost touch.

And what became of the Double D? One day quite a bit later as I was cruising up the waterway, I spotted her grounded on the side of the east bank. I never did find out exactly how and why that came about, but after a few weeks some angry denizen of the waterway had painted a message on her side in big white letters.

It said, "Get this piece of shit out of here."

CHAPTER 44

The General

ONE OF THE MOST cherished memories from my VA days was an acquaintance with General James Vaught. The day we met I was already behind in my work schedule at the VA clinic. I saw that the General was on my list and waiting patiently in the lobby for his initial appointment. It seemed to me to be appropriate to go out and find him in the waiting area. Then I could escort him personally to my office rather than keep him waiting longer for my nurse to fetch him. He certainly deserved that small modicum of respectful consideration.

He had not asked for, nor expected, any special treatment but I sensed that this little gesture of respect touched him deeply and we immediately bonded with each other. In the coming months he would let himself into the hallway of exam rooms that led to my office and I would hear the rap of a cane on my door. I was usually talking with one of the patients when I heard the familiar sound. Opening the door, I saw his strong handsome eighty-something year old face beneath his cap and its three shiny silver stars. Those stars,

I swear, they looked as big to me as a chrome bumper on a 1950's Dodge. I would ask my patient if he would mind if the General joined us for some conversation. Invariably, they were delighted at the prospect and he would come in, sit down and chat....and for a few minutes all three of us would unwind, forget the pressures and tedium of the clinic and recall army stories or we would talk about how we could improve the service for the Veterans, maybe start a housing project and a local rehab facility for severely disabled Vets.

General Vaught was a great man and one of the few I have met with strong personal charisma. He quickly became a father figure and mentor to me. I had observed the effect he had on others and it was remarkable. You could see their eyes light up with admiration and respect.

He was a natural leader who at one time had been in command of all the troops in South Korea and had been a central strategic figure at the Pentagon. He would proudly tell you he was a direct descendent of Francis Marion, the legendary guerrilla commander of the American Revolution known as the Swamp Fox. Marion had operated back then around the local South Carolina swamps evading the wrath of the despised Colonel Tarleton and his merciless British calvary. General Vaught claimed there was a genetic basis for his ascension to the command of the Delta Force, then the epitome of our special forces units.

I grasped more fully how this man had affected our nation when I attended his funeral. Sadly, he had drowned after a boating accident on a local pond. The ceremony was in the beautiful and spacious Tilly Swamp Baptist church on a back road just north of Conway South Carolina, the town where he was born. There were at least a thousand mourners from all across the country, indeed from all

around the world. Finely decorated senior officers and ordinary ser-
vicemen in the uniforms of many nations joined the civilians that
filled the hall.

In speech after speech his accomplishments and heroism in battle
were recounted by those who had served with him. What I found
most remarkable was that every speaker felt about him the same way
I did. Each description revealed an aspect of the man as I had known
him. This, no doubt, was the result of a lifetime of consistent character and it engendered love and respect from those who knew him.
Though they were all strangers to me, except for his lovely wife Flor-
ence, all in attendance seemed to have the same regard for this local
giant, this modest, heroic man.

We all sang *The Battle Hymn of The Republic* as one voice. Never
had the lyrics affected me as they did on that day. We followed his
coffin to the gravesite and after the honor guard fired the ceremonial
rounds into the air, they laid his flag-draped casket down into his
grave as the old Baptist hymn *All Is Well With My Soul* spontaneously
filled the air. I never heard music like that before or since. It was
as if a chorus of angels were singing in perfect harmony with voices
coming from around and above me. Music floated in the air, weight-
less and suspended. I can't explain it, but it surrounded me. I joined
the singing and it blended into a most beautiful celestial tribute to
his passing.

CHAPTER 45

No Where To Run But A
Good Time To Hide

AFTER I CASHED IN my chips at the VA, I spent some years wandering in the professional desert so to speak. I tried my hand as a civilian physician at the Navy and then at the Air Force. The providers and hospital staff worked diligently and with great dedication. They were tireless in keeping the service members mission-ready and tending to their families and retirees. I was honored to serve on these teams who cared for the nation's defenders.

But being a contractor and not an employee, I served at the whims of a cadre of remote number crunchers. They were not necessarily impressed with the value of a very thorough but relatively slow practitioner willing to stay and provide stability to their staff.

At the Air Force, the managers tended to overwork and rotate a succession of constantly dissatisfied temporary replacements. Once again, when high turnover caused shortages of providers, it created severe stress for the staff that remained. Though they were often overwhelmed, those who stalwartly remained were required to take up the slack caring for patient panels that had been left unattended by the manpower vacuums. This is an efficient formula to destroy morale. It was made all the worse by many long months of multiple unfilled vacancies. It was an all too familiar recollection of my VA experience. I knew where this professional road was headed and I was not equipped to thrive in such an environment.

Making matters worse, we had become so dependent on the computer for the entire patient record that it was almost impossible to function without it. When the system went down, you were essentially dead in the water. Despite this handicap, apparently no one in management gave thought to reducing the patient load for that day and rescheduling non emergent care for another time when the computers were up and functioning. Often these outrageous conditions continued for several days at a time. To think of the many billions of dollars that had been spent by the government to produce such an unreliable digital system was maddening. That no one had made effective plans to function properly in the event of its failure was unforgivable.

It was an excellent recipe for a peptic ulcer and behavior like this gave me serious qualms about the future of government run healthcare.

Yet beyond the military, the country was crying out for a system that would serve all its citizens fairly, a mission our traditional formats had obviously failed to provide. It seemed likely that to control costs and extend the benefits of modern medicine to rich and poor alike, some sort of a national health service would eventually emerge. With it would come more guidelines, rules, laws and reimbursement schemes to organize and monitor its implementation. Under these circumstances, the focus between the doctor and patient was in danger of fading even further into distant memory. May the idealistic fresh faces of the future remember that they work for the patient and not the payor, that they are engaged in a sacred trust..

Eventually I found a venue that allowed me to breathe a bit more easily. I began taking temporary work assignments with private practices that needed help to bridge gaps when personnel left or practices grew. Because I was just passing through and relieving shortages, there was greater latitude for me to function unimpeded and the patients appreciated greatly the time and intensity of the thorough evaluations they were receiving. The practices were the direct recipients of the help and were grateful for the assistance. There was no impersonal bureaucracy making value judgements.

Evolving events revealed that there was no lack of dedication or physical courage in the hearts of the current cadre of medical workers. Covid 19 held up that mirror. The rush into the breach without hesitation, despite the despicable lack of reliable personal protective equipment and the subsequent risks of mortal danger, dramatically revealed the heroism of the entire healthcare workforce.

Our nurses and nurse's aides, God bless them, underpaid and overworked, constantly exposed through their intimate patient contact, the respiratory technicians helping manage the airway issues of patients infected with the insanely contagious and deadly airborne virus, the radiology team, the lab techs who drew blood and collected other biological specimens, all the workers in the healthcare field from management to dietary and maintenance, who came in each day and kept the wheels turning. No one had signed up for their job thinking it might kill them.

Yet our brave countrymen responded without fail, like soldiers responding to the call to duty. It revealed the reservoir of nobility that remains in our society, the capability of the average citizen. Their tireless and compassionate struggle to care for the crushing volume of critically ill patients played out endlessly across our TV screens.

This bravery gave me a great deal of pride in my colleagues and hope for the coming years. Such heroes emboldened the nation to face the grave challenges before us while our self-obsessed President did his best to pretend that the danger would disappear even as the casualties rose exponentially. In this calamity he made a mockery of wearing masks and avoiding social behaviors that would prevent disease transmission. Perhaps he needed to spend a few nights at the bedside caring for an overwhelming patient load that was dying before his eyes to realize that prevention was a better idea than treatment. I got the impression he just didn't care about it. Cleaning up the mess was somebody else's problem.

CHAPTER 46

But I Digress

AT THE OUTSET OF my story, I had told you about the new homestead Lisa and I had bought on St Helena Island, South Carolina. That was in 2019. I planned to retire from medicine and looked forward to continuing my writing.

My lifetime had traversed through a most fortunate and prosperous period in the long parade of human experience. Those years had many novel and comfortable qualities. Undreamt of technologies and amusements had become common place. There had been political stability so strong that it seemed unshakably established. You might call this post-World War II era the *Pax Americana,* the American Peace. Though this term is bound to offend many a critic, there certainly is some truth to it.

That edifice had started to radically shift over the last three years and the polarity of global and domestic political order had begun to totter unpredictably. Our relationship to NATO and thus our focus on Europe as our core strategic priority had come into doubt. China was rising, Russia was asserting itself. Now there was a new sense of uncertainty in the air. Liberal democracy and globalism seemed to be losing ground while nationalistic authoritarian impulses were brewing.

I could imagine a future when the comforts, freedom and relative safety that we had enjoyed might seem like just a distant memory. Our progeny would look back upon our times and reflect upon its lessons. One intriguing question that would be fair to ask: why, despite all the advantages of an age such as ours, could personal happiness and spiritual peace seem so elusive for so many?

I was holding fast the gleanings I had gathered on my life's journey so far. I was determined not to psychically scatter in my advancing age but to continue to concentrate my focus on this changing world and to evolve spiritually. That was my intention when I opened the gate and entered our five acres of sanctuary to begin my retirement.

CHAPTER 47

Conversation With Zhivago

DESPITE THE CONTINUOUS CASCADE of political turbulence that had been an everyday occurrence since the 2016 Presidential electoral season and inauguration, the first seven months on our island of sanity passed pleasantly. My daughter Viena, her husband Jacob (who is like a son to me) and their three beautiful children were fifteen minutes away. We rarely had other visitors and that was fine with us. On Halloween my wife put up a plastic skeleton on the porch and we joked that that was the last Trick or Treater who had dared to come up our driveway. I settled into my literary tasks organizing 40 years of poems. I was now writing prose to make the poetry more accessible to others.

Then came March 2020 and the Covid 19 invasion.

Given our advancing ages, Lisa and I became functional recluses as we oldsters were at greatest risks of dying in the pandemic. Suddenly the entire nation was affected by the rapid advance of the deadly threat. I rarely left my property. I had plenty of time on my hands.

At night I enjoyed imagining meeting great minds and sensibilities. We had a 32-foot RV trailer set up on the property and I liked to spend time there, particularly at night, contemplating existence. Sometimes I would conjure up the memory of some bright luminary who had passed on centuries ago, sometimes the living, sometimes a fictional character. One rainy night, as the hot southern wind was rocking my trailer slightly with the mild threat that a tropical storm brings, I felt strangely comfortable and relaxed. I thought this would be a really good time to get Yuri Zhivago's take on some of life's perennial existential challenges.

After all, he had been ripped from the moorings of his privileged life by the whirlwinds of World War I. Then followed the October Revolution and, on its heels, the Russian Civil War. He became irretrievably separated from his family and lover. Finally, he was able to flee the carnage and upheaval that surrounded him only to become a hungry and freezing fugitive. Despite the social dislocation, the degradation of the value of human life, the wholesale murder, despite all of the horror and deprivation swirling about him, this gentle soul retained the capacity to write poetry extolling the glory of love and the beauty of this planet.

If you were thrust into such a vortex of cultural confusion, would you still know your center, your spiritual core? Or, like so many, would you be disoriented without the defining nature of your occupation, social position and your possessions. That is the challenge Zhivago overcame and though confronted by the depths of horror, he still strove to nurture that which is beautiful and life affirming in the human soul.

As a physician and a poet, he had been given a very special vantage point to observe and understand the human condition, to intervene when possible and alleviate the pain and suffering that has always challenged humanity. This poem expressed my longing to meet him in the impossible ether of the heart and mind:

Yuri,
I called to you tonight
Across the white expansive wilderness of time
Wandering intellect, passionate soul
I was wishing that we both might be
At once together
Seeing the Earth
Breathing

In the warm spring's light
At our ease
We might speak of the nature of man
Looking far past the epidermis
To marvel at the depths of marrow

And then,
Reemerging into brilliant day
The world in its magnificence
Splashed across our senses
Our beings borne down a flowered road
Laughing
Hand upon shoulder
We might pass in phantom glory

HE SEEMED SO FAR away. The distance... the interminable walk across the snow- blown steppe...the dislocation in time and space between the two of us....the impassible gap between life and fiction. I would imagine calling out to him in the night as if we could overcome these barriers between us, to be together, both living, happy to see each other. My imagination yielded a fantastic illusion of contact.

"Hello Yuri," I said with a smile, "you're looking good considering all you've been through."

"Good to see you too," Yuri said, his eyes brightening.

He cocked his head sightly, "Isn't the resilient capacity of the human heart to bear the unbearable and still reemerge to bloom, isn't it a wonder?" he asked.

"Yes," I mused, "in some ways you might think such an impulse is driven by nature but in the case of human beings it also entails conscious choices. That is the key, I think. When events gather like storms carrying all before them into an uncertain and dangerous future we may only steer with our tiny rudders upon the roiling sea of destiny and do the best we can. Our free will intent on virtue and a heart open to beauty and kindness bent against a violent wind... that is an inspiring image to contemplate. If I may, that is how I think of you, Yuri Andreievich."

"You are very kind my friend," he said.

"I think you will agree that we both have been most fortunate to have practiced medicine," I said.

"Yes," said Yuri, "it's a place to fight a good fight. Always do your best in the interest of your patient and you will sleep well at night."

"That is true," said I, "it is a fine workplace for a poet and a lover of beauty. The joy of seeing the lame walking, the dying recovering, the blind given back their sight. This is not just business as usual.

The poet's eye catches all this from an exquisitely privileged vantage point. He can be an artist at this work, not one who simply monitors the outcomes of his clinical interventions, not just a functionary who applies practical solutions to mechanical problems. The proper care of another human being demands that you embrace the spiritual presence of your patient as you wrestle with the physical realities of disease...all the while you must struggle to relieve suffering with your wits and the scientific tools at your command. It invites the roles of the shaman and the priest to aid the scientific technician. "

Yuri nodded slightly with approval. Placing his hand to his chin and then pointing his finger with a shake, he said earnestly, "When just the physician and a dying soul are alone together there can come a rare and precious moment...no thought being given to future concerns. It approaches a pure offering. It is an intimacy that no other person will ever see or will likely ever know about. This is a challenge for the poet, to find the right words, to offer a soothing touch, to give the look of empathy and the sounds of comfort. At such a moment as this, the hair on the back of your neck might stand up and you might feel a chill running up your spine for you have touched the threshold of the holy."

I just listened. He knew I was well aware of how it felt to look at life and medicine that way.

"You know," he finally added, "I started out reading books, listening to lectures and looking at hidden worlds under my microscope. My practice at first seemed a challenge, but still the world seemed to be in reasonable order. But then I was cast out into a world of utter chaos with human drama so devastating that I was forced to fight against spiritual drowning, from being overwhelmed. There were long months of gasping for air, consumed by the struggle to survive.

But I always believed I was surviving to live a life worthy of living again, and, in the end, that was my salvation."

I grinned and digested what I had heard.

"Have you given thought as to what you would want to become of your poems?" Zhivago asked with a smile. "What is your ambition for them?"

"Well, to hear my work discussed in the cafes of Crete or Cyprus...or Athens...now that would be a crown of laurel leaves I would proudly wear. And in centuries to come I would want someone to draw inspiration from them. That they might recognize a kindred spirit and by connecting with my thoughts and feelings the poems might convey the embers of my being. That I might leave a worthwhile message. Those are my ambitions."

"I have always found it interesting and odd," said I, "that in a world intricately connected by the ties of sophisticated communication, most people fail to see the truly big changes coming. How could the collapse of the Soviet Union come as a surprise to so many people? That is truly astounding, but it is not atypical. When world order is upended in spectacular collapses, when the paradigms shift, people are often shocked by the changes."

Yuri spoke up, "So true. After all the Russian people had been through. The First World War with the Germans and Austrians, the troubles with the Czar and the devastation of the Revolution, the Civil War and then what ...Stalin?...then Hitler? Unimaginable suffering and cruelty in that century precipitated by the Great War of 1914 that no one saw coming in the first place."

"I was born after all that," I said "the dust was still settling. I was very lucky, very lucky indeed. For that I say, 'Thank you Lord for all Your blessings and may I be worthy'."

"Amen," said Yuri.

I continued, "With poetry I am striving for depth and clarity, for a foundation upon which to build an impression of an organized point of view and an exposition of feeling, as honest a rendition as possible and with themes and purpose that are worthy of the effort. So far it has often been a very lonely literary journey. I try to remember that regardless of eventual recognition or confinement to obscurity, it is the work that is important. Out of a lack of self-consciousness some of the best creative work will be born."

"I think you are on a promising path." said Zhivago.

That made my night.

CHAPTER 48

Nighttime Meditation
With Plutarch

ON ANOTHER BLUSTERY EVENING, I thought it would be a really good time to get Plutarch's opinion on some pressing current matters. That great intellect was a Greek biographer, philosopher and essayist who was born in 46 AD, a time when Rome ruled his country. He is best remembered as the author of *Parallel Lives* pairing illustrious Greeks with Romans, comparing their mutual virtues and vices.

Plutarch that night was thinking of some new parallel lives but rejected the pairing of Hitler and Trump. He considered this briefly given their cynical emergence through a democratic process and their reputation for lackadaisical work habits, but he found that the latter had no grip on an organized ideology or control of the military beyond that granted by constitutional authority. Rather, Plutarch praised the American Constitution itself, as it did not grant the emergency powers needed to suspend civil liberties indefinitely. That was the keyhole that Hitler crawled through to create his dictatorship out of the young, weak and inexperienced Weimar Republic of 1933. Indeed, the lack of such a device in the American document may have been the main impediment that had held another whirlwind in check. In the end, the wisdom of the American Founders seems to have made the difference.

Plutarch was reminded of Sparta and the centuries of stability and power that emanated from their constitution. This, according to tradition, was promulgated by the law-giver Lycurgus and prevailed for many centuries. The Spartan culture was completely focused on maintaining military supremacy and their constitution laid out the social blueprint to accomplish this.

Plutarch noted how America had focused far beyond the all-consuming societal goal of maintaining order and military might. The American Founders incorporated the Athenian democratic innovation, their love of freedom and self-expression, and then blended it all with the post-Enlightenment enshrinement of the sanctity of the individual. Indeed, they idealized this credo and legally protected it from the intrusion of the State.

Of course, Plutarch saw the warts and shallowness of the initial American effort. It had limited the exalted status of full liberty to white men. But it was a damn good start in his opinion. He was thinking well of the ongoing American experiment even though he was all too familiar with the fragility of the evolving institutions.

I thought about this awhile. Hitler was certainly a mesmerizing actor on a stage that had grown ever larger until the performance became the collective reality.

Trump was also a consummate showman. Part carnival barker, part snake oil salesman, he excelled in the performance of illusions. Card tricks, the shell game, he did them all with finesse and credible sleight of hand. He had a touch of Liberace in his grand entrances and hints at pageantry. His magic act was highlighted by demonstrations of hypnosis that he employed upon large swaths of his audience. Rather than relying on soothing words in a darkened room and swinging pocket watches, he worked with flashing shiny objects and psychic misdirection. One did have to admit, that when his performance was over, he managed to maintain a grip on a large portion of his audience. He could alter their behavior and channel their thoughts and prejudices in such a way that helped him accomplish his selfish goals. That put him in Hitler territory, maybe just. Hitler-lite one might call him.

"How about the pairing of Trump and Alcibiades? Now there's a duo with something in common...charisma and serial betrayal," I mused.

Plutarch thought a moment, and just smiled with a nod. At that point he felt he had said enough and was gone.

Alcibiades and Trump. That was an intriguing comparison of parallel lives. The Athenian had been born in the Golden Age of Athens and raised as an orphan in the household of the wealthy and powerful Pericles who was a pivotal figure in Athens' sudden and profound blossoming during the century following the repulsion of the Persian invasions.

Alcibiades was wealthy, he was extremely handsome and intelligent. He was famously vain. He had won Olympic athletic honors and possessed a magnetic charisma that propelled him to a stellar political career. His oratorical skills were famous (here he differed from the Donald most glaringly).

He became a leading voice in the Athenian Assembly where his speeches bent the political arc of his nation...always toward the objects of his unbridled ambitions...and ultimately toward disaster. He betrayed his own City State when he had felt threatened by his fellow citizens. He defected to Sparta and divulged decisive military secrets to the enemy that were instrumental in the defeat of the Athenian invasion forces in Sicily.

Despite this, years later he was called back by the Athenians in their vain attempt to ward off total defeat by Sparta and her allies. The depth of this diseased love affair with such a duplicitous character came to serve as a measure of the degree of desperation that had descended upon Athens and its faded dream of empire.

Alcibiades and Trump, these two brothers of the charismatic were not just symptomatic of their times, they were both transformational characters. They were the yeast that had to be added lest the bread of history not rise. Or at least that is my less than humble opinion.

All this brought to mind an essay and a poem I had written years before. It now was ringing with new echoes. In part, it was a cautionary tale of the dangerous mesmerizing mixture of reckless charisma and greed in a national leader. It was a warning to beware of unbridled narcissism and self-interest because it invites betrayal. This brought Mr. Trump into sharp focus beneath the lens of history. He was by no means alone in this despicable club and the damage he would inflict on his country's future was still far from clear.

CHAPTER 49

The Athenian Fleet Is
Defeated, 413 BC

In his great *History of the Peloponnesian War*, Thucydides wrote contemporaneously of the events of the epic military struggle between the Athenian and Spartan alliances. In one phase of the war, a huge Athenian and allied naval force carrying an army of invasion sailed for Sicily. They intended to subdue the rich and powerful city of Syracuse.

This expedition was motivated more by a lust for greed than strategic necessity but the Assembly of Athens was persuaded to proceed principally by the charismatic Alcibiades. Just before departure, some persons carried out an act of sacrilege by overturning statues of the god Hermes. Hermes served as messenger to the Olympian gods. The religious and superstitious Athenians were shocked and outraged by this event and there was a great sense of foreboding that the venture would be doomed to disaster as a consequence. Regardless, the armada sailed for Sicily.

There was considerable suspicion that one of the generals with the invasion force, Alcibiades himself, was responsible for the desecration. Ships were sent to overtake the fleet and return him to Athens to stand trial for his life but Alcibiades fled before he could be taken. He made his way to Sparta to become an extremely damaging military advisor against his fellow Athenians.

The fleet landed in Sicily and the army was at first successful under the command of an elderly but steadfast and skillful general named Nicias. He suffered, we are told, from painful kidney stones. He was able to bring his army to the brink of defeating the Syracusans and taking their city. But ultimately, he was unable to complete his blockade and siege.

It became apparent that he must withdraw his army rapidly to avoid being overwhelmed. He was prepared to evacuate by sea when a lunar eclipse occurred. Nicias interpreted this as an omen forbidding him to leave at that moment. While he waited, the Syracusans seized the opportunity and launched a surprising and devastating naval attack on the Athenian Fleet. Nicias and his troops watched helplessly in horror as their navy was decimated.

Now, with no chance for withdrawal or resupply, it was obvious that the army was in imminent peril. They made an attempt to break out into open country but were cut off and all were killed or captured.

Nicias was taken as a captive before the enemy generals. He knew some of these men from earlier days and these were inclined to spare his life, knowing him to be an honorable man. But others were intent on eliminating him and, with these men prevailing, Nicias was summarily put to death.

The other troops in his army were not as fortunate. They were imprisoned in a stone quarry and forced to endure stifling heat, starvation and complete lack of sanitation. They perished painfully or were sold into slavery. With this defeat, Athens began a long decline which finally ended in her capture by the Spartans in 404 BC.

Today most would likely ascribe the fate of the Athenians to an ignorance of astronomy and the superstitious nature of Nicias driving him to make his fatal error of judgement. Despite his rational insight into most matters and his clear understanding of the military imperatives, he betrayed his instinct to flee. But to the contemporaries of Nicias and Thucydides, brilliant men by acclaim, the forces at work were far more mysterious. The omens were multilayered and ominous. Surely the guilt of hubris for this unnecessary and risky adventure loomed heavy on their minds. The desecration of their sacred images cried out for retribution.

We who think we know better today might step back and ponder further. Even in our modern empirical age, the interplay between free will and the circumstances that surround us continues to be uncertain. Religion and rational analysis continue to vie in our attempt to understand the drivers of destiny.

Thucydides had touched on the elements of myth as it approaches the horizon of the mysterious. For those who profess to know the will of God, who are the chosen and who are not, the world and its purposes seem to be clear and comprehensible. History would seem to argue against certitude.

THE ATHENIAN FLEET IS DEFEATED, 413 BC
(View from the Beach)

Nicias
Captain of men
Interpreter of omens
So worn and weary when swallowed up
Not far from the gates of Syracuse.

How nearly he had flown
But for the darkened moon
That seemed to speak of certain death
But never told for whom
Not until this moment
Of oars and men consumed.

Nicias
Eagle-minded man
Racked with pain
Haunted by the image of Hermes overturned
You have hovered by the water's edge
And now must bear sad witness to your ruin.
Soon you will pray for pity
But feel the angry stone
Against your cheek.

Was it Fate that drove the wheel that day
Or the frailty of man?

Who can say what forces work
When instincts are betrayed.

CHAPTER 50

Swimming Underwater

THE SUMMER SUN IS intense in the low country of South Carolina. You need to do your chores in the morning before it gets unbearably hot. Even so I would sweat through my clothes just mowing the lawn. In such a setting, access to a swimming pool is transformational, an oasis of comfort in a beautiful but blistering scenario.

My beloved pool had come with the property. I hadn't appreciated the value of this feature. I thought, "that's a nice little extra". A useful something that just happened to be thrown into the bargain. Wrong. The pool became an essential treasure to protect, like air conditioning or plumbing. It became an object of love.

I would swim every day except when there was lightning. We had a nice wooden deck that led from our bedroom to the pool. It was an above the ground aquatic refuge, 32 feet in diameter and a bit over 4 feet in depth. A 12-foot cantilevered market umbrella created a movable zone of shade on the water.

You could swim a bit on the surface but I was drawn to that middle zone between the surface and the bottom. Not only was I shielded from the heat by the warm water but I noticed the silence, the peace, the weightlessness and ease of movement swimming under the surface.

When the grandkids came to swim, I would lay on the poolside chaise lounge with music playing, a book and a drink. The shade of the umbrella made the heat tolerable. There I would act as a lifeguard, watching happiness break out in the pool as the kids invented games, splashing and playing with wide-opened eyes and laughing. This modest oasis was worth its weight in gold on a hot day.

When I was alone, I was increasingly drawn to swimming underwater in silent solitude. One must break the surface like any mammal to catch a breath, but I became more eager to linger longer and longer below, inhabiting the depths as best I could. It was good exercise and fun but there was more at work here. I felt sheltered.

One day things became clarified and the meaning of the metaphor struck me: surrounded by woods and hidden from view, serene silence was the strata I was seeking. I was hiding from the viral plague but also evading engagement with the unstable political chaos that was gripping America. In truth I was hiding from the challenges that were confronting the world at large. But it was becoming untenable to remain submerged.

I was free to seek oxygen any time I wished and to alight from the water. Now with the fires of the presidential election igniting anger and fear, the surface was compelling my attention. Things were happening that I could no longer view from a distance. It was time that I must break my silence and try to combat the lies and propaganda that were being bantered about.

I started by confronting some of my Facebook friends who were enthralled by Trump, but I found them to be implacable. Not only were they impressed by the torrent of his lies, but they propagated them with repetition and elaboration on their posts. It seemed as if there was some posthypnotic suggestion at work that caused the susceptible to ignore Trump's obvious prevarications, his manipulations and his dangerous assault on the foundations of democracy. He had been impeached, mishandled the pandemic, gutted Federal agencies of qualified professionals and appointed unqualified political cronies to sensitive positions in their places. None of this seemed to rattle the true believers. It seemed as if they had become completely blind to the dangers that this aberrant President posed.

I tried to reason, through private messaging, and express my fears and concerns about this troubling political descent toward authoritarianism with some of these friends and respected colleagues. When pressed with my assertion that many of these folks were doing the work of the Russians by reposting lies and distortions, the response from the most intellectual of this group was:

"We will use any weapons necessary. I won't let my grandchildren grow up in a world run by liberals"

There was a real sense of desperation in his voice. This I found dangerous and frightening. It was very sad for me to see how little I could budge anyone from their unassailable commitment to this demagogue, this purveyor of falsehood and prejudice. To my ears, the assault on truth was an eerie echo of Goebbels and the Bolsheviks, a potential trajectory into totalitarianism. The descent into mass murder from that transition was still a vivid vision within the memory of the living.

I had been too long swimming underwater where order and harmony were not disturbed. It was becoming necessary to speak out in the clear light of day.

I thought of Albert Camus and the context of his spiritual and philosophical struggles, his progress, both before and after World War II.

His novel *The Plague* came into focus. The concurrence of pandemic and political volatility made comparisons with present times compelling but the differences were glaring between his realities and mine. We were each a product of our time and those times differed distinctly. I thought of a poem I had written around 1992 that was taking on new relevance in these dark days.

CHAPTER 51

Of Seasons And Titans
(Circa 1992)

WHEN THIS POEM WAS written, life seemed quite stable and secure. Of course, there was turbulence and countless personal tragedies including limited wars and the specter of nuclear holocaust. But overall, there was a widespread sense of security and the continuity of routine rarely enjoyed by others throughout history. It was easy to be lulled into a belief that normality and order would persist. But change has always been in the offing as one epoch slowly dims and the new one emerges.

The subtle clues as to what the shifting paradigm will bring are evident in retrospect but seem mysterious at first, like a distant storm faintly discernible only to the most acutely aware. Often even these keen observers can only sense that change is approaching but not its detail nor its character. It is only when events are upon us and it is obvious that the present has been fundamentally transformed that the general public becomes aware how destiny has revealed its new realities.

1

Beneath the soft belly of this vast blue sky
Woven through the hissing summer heat
Threads the trace of a distant plaintive cry
That the hounds of epoch howl
A portent faint yet clear
And the clash that they foretell titanic
Upon the iceberg of perception
Is drawing ever near

2

Fate
Great leveler
Your face concealed beyond our view
From here
Where the monuments are effaced in the acrid air
And the human faces weather
Rapt with their mortal cares
Drawn in their cycles to the earth
Forming the fertile ash
That haunts with expectation
The ground that bears the coming of an Age

3

Ideas
Irresistible ideas whose time have come

That bind to living forms
Flesh into action
Fasten to the day
And take on the name of Now,
A bright mirage of seamless continuity
That blurs the minds of men
Singing with a siren's song
Of summer without end
Still the wheel of epoch casts a changeling light
And with its newborn rays
Traces of the coming dawn
Mingle with the full-blown day

4

The hounds of epoch howl foretelling
The titanic clash upon the iceberg of perception
They call out to us
Shrieking on the freezing night wind
There on the dark heaving sea
Now unmistakable
At the moment the impact begins

CHAPTER 52

Thinking Of Camus
July 28, 2020

He was raised in the French Algerian port of Oran, his world rent from its axis by the Nazi conquest of the metropolitan homeland. He had been an advocate of the oppressed Algerian Arabs before the war and had become somewhat famous with his countrymen. He returned to France and joined the Resistance at the risk of his life.

Emerging from that communal humiliation and torture, Camus wrestled with the specter of absurdity in a world that, for him, held no God or afterlife. His novel, *The Plague*, begins with the narrator observing keenly, almost clinically, the city of Oran; its bland life, its diverting habits and its drab physical structure. The town is described in exacting detail down to the dry dust on the hot walls. Against this backdrop, Doctor Rieux kicks away a dead rat with a bloody maw that he has encountered on his doorstep. This odd and curious anomaly portends the coming plague.

Dead rats, that ancient harbinger of pestilence and dread, who can ignore their presence when they appear on the streets? Even when the cause and the danger they represent are not clear, a reaction seems imperative. Camus did not shrink from the exigencies of his time; he focused on them and confronted them. He was keenly observant and was inspired to act.

I, in contrast, have been most comfortable swimming beneath the surface of the waters, though I am aware of grave danger in the atmosphere above. Optimism gives me a peaceful respite, the blurring of details gives a quiet relief. In fact, it seems to obliterate details. Camus and I have adopted different lenses through which to view our worlds. I do not perceive myself as a captive of the absurd. I do not profess to know whether God exists or does not exist. Hope remains cherished. The openness to imagine spiritual transcendence is not a weakness to me but a strength; it amplifies my life rather than diminishes it. In these regards I diverge fundamentally from Camus.

In truth, I have been observing events from afar, here in my quiet reserve. Who can deny that now there is mortal danger emerging around us. The times are calling passionately for action, to break the silence. But what can be done?

There is grave danger in the air
Camus is observant down to minutia
Surveying the details of the town of Oran

I have been swimming underwater
Gliding in the silence
Not wanting to hear the din
But the peace has been disturbed
And I have heard an urgent cry
Coming from above:
"Break through to the surface
Can't you see
The rats are upon the streets!"

I breach the waves to hear
The hounds of epoch howl
Their portents now are loud and clear
And the clash that they foretold titanic
Upon the iceberg of perception
Is drawing ever near

Most surely we'll be forced to act
When Destiny reveals its face
In a flood that drives us with its tide
A paltry rudder in our hand
To mitigate the savage swells
That tear and tumble through our land

CHAPTER 53

A Tale Of Two Cities
August 7, 2020

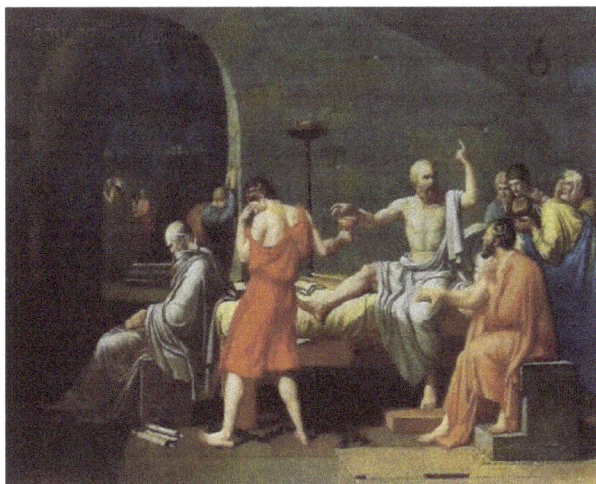

THE TEMPO OF MY passion for expression quickened and the outrage I felt for the abandonment of the search for truth in the national discourse intensified. For without the ability to come to a consensus on the nature of reality how can a free people make responsible decisions to navigate the challenges of communal life. I thought of Socrates and his unflagging devotion to the search for truth, his fearless commitment to that goal even at the cost of his life. Athens had been conquered by the Spartan Alliance and its citizens were desperate in their humiliation to punish the sources of their weakness. They fell upon the purveyor of "corrupting new ideas."

Socrates was offered retreat,
He refused to escape the hemlock
He said he was old and would not leave his city
That city of condemnation and sorrow

He would not defy its laws, its swirling body politic
Desperate to regain its feet
Fumbling and striking back.

At what?
This secular saint
This giant of philosophy
This man that gently embraced his dying moments
Discussing the search for truth with the great minds
Of his friends?

There is a time when we must speak up
The timid and the wary
Though the wolves of prejudice might lurk
And the knock on the door might come
There is a time when we must speak up
For Truth

CHAPTER 54

Sheltered In Place
August 15, 2020

THE NATIONAL TEMPERATURE WAS rising. Hopes for a summertime reprieve from the pandemic had faded and this portended a horrible prognosis for the coming winter when it was likely to careen out of control unless decisive public health measures were imposed. Even then, it would likely be a battle with mass casualties in the hundreds of thousands.

At the heart of this calamity, President Trump sat like a spider in his web waiting to feed on a preserved economy that would propel him to another term in the November election. He chose to pretend that the pandemic would disappear. At least that was the fantasy he promoted. Meanwhile the staggering death toll mounted.

He mocked the basic sanitary measures of wearing masks and social distancing. He wanted to create the mirage that the life of the nation would not be substantially changed by this virus, a mere cousin of the flu he intimated. He wanted to open our economy and rush to return to the sense of normality we had known in February of 2020. Yet we were not close to having a handle on the public health emergency.

This was perhaps the cruelest lie of his long deceitful career. It became clear that his reelection prospects, not the health of the nation he led, was his highest priority. He was more than willing to sacrifice the lives of untold numbers of his constituents to achieve his nefarious ends. But how was it possible for him to throttle the public health experts and enlist the silence of the Republican Party in this selfish quest? Where were we headed?

Neighbors once had carried embers of fire in winter to their neighbors' homes to light their hearths. There is dignity in being a tiny Prometheus, a flashing light in the sky of existence. It was important to be prepared to serve such a purpose especially if events were to careen into the chaos and savagery that mankind was heir to.

Now my reports were to come in real time. I was alert and back from the shadows. I had left the company of the ancient Greeks. Now I was at the front lines with my fellow citizens. So many were struggling to simply get by, to survive this catastrophe.

Lisa and I were committed to surviving and to flourish again regardless of the challenges. Our little sanctuary on this barrier island in the heart of Gullah country would be our salvation. We would not forget who we had already become.

Where to begin?
I think therefore I am
Yes, that is a good place to start
And I will affirm that life is precious
And that I embrace the world
This world that my senses have shown me
This world of sublime beauty and unspeakable sorrow
A place of great harvest and great loss

Now I am seventy
And outside my walls the world seems to tremble
The pleasant silence has been rudely disturbed
Pestilence and confusion are seen running wild
The tolling of bells is constantly heard
Everywhere souls are seeking asylum
As chaos is prowling
To feed on the lie

And I,

I cling to my beautiful Lisa, my Lara
Taking refuge together here in the wild
Surrounded by lushness and the soothing of nature
We live on an island where spirits may thrive

It is a fine place to work at becoming Zhivago
To feel his emotions
To see through moist eyes
That even beneath a cruel Russian winter
Though snowbound and hidden
Profusions of flowers in Spring will arise

I RESOLVED TO USE this time of isolation to write a book. I would speak unequivocally to the world and report on my times as events occurred. We did not know where this disorder would lead. Lord, keep us from spiraling into the depths of horror. We had seen that movie play out in the few years before my birth. The great Western barrier reef against despotism had been holding out so far. It was not yet a time for panic. Heightened vigilance was appropriate.

CHAPTER 55

The Spectacle Unfolds
November 3, 2020

IT HAD SEEMED TO be an interminable summer and fall. The mishandling of the pandemic had needlessly caused tens of thousands of deaths. The Trump administration had tried to hobble the Postal Service in an attempt to limit voter turnout. This would force people to risk infection in order to vote in person. Was this the height of cynicism? He claimed in advance that fraudulent voting would be inevitable on a large scale due to the shift toward the mail-in ballot. It was an obvious attempt to undermine the legitimacy of any result that didn't favor Mr. Donald.

Finally, the day of decision arrived in America. The election was underway. The first shock of the evening was the absence of the hoped for game changing Democratic victories in Congress and the development of a seesaw battle in the presidential race. Due to the fact that the overwhelming number of mail-in ballots were for Biden and the larger proportion of Trump's votes were cast in person on election day, it appeared Trump might be leading on election night.

In the wee hours after election day, Trump declared victory and predictably professed the occurrence of widespread voter fraud, though he did not produce any supporting evidence. The result of the election was far from decided but you knew that if he lost, Trump's legal challenges would soon begin...with all the resources of the Executive Branch and the bully pulpit at his disposal.

Would facts finally matter??

CHAPTER 56

November 4, 2020

MORNING ARRIVED AND OUR nerves were shot. All night long Lisa and I had watched the election results come in. We could not believe what we were seeing. I had expected a blue wave of revulsion to express just how angry and disappointed we were as the American People. That finally we would rise up in our righteous indignation to declare to the world that we were still a nation dedicated to resisting autocracy. That truth was a virtue and political repression was a sin. That our better angels would prevail and we would address an agenda of systemic inequities and strive to excise the legacies of racism.

How shocking it was to see the hard truths revealed by ciphers on a TV screen. The Republicans had actually gained in the House, though still a minority, and the control of the Senate was in serious doubt. Trump had garnered over 70,000,000 votes. It revealed the rising prominence of ugly instincts that could easily unleash the more savage and destructive impulses of humanity. Half the nation stood declaring itself unwilling to embrace the future that the pollsters had predicted and so many of us had hoped for. It foreshadowed the persistence of a forceful Trumpist movement regardless of the final election outcome.

It was true that Trump supporters could tout the low price of gasoline and historically low mortgage rates, how the economy had surged before the pandemic, how Isis had disappeared, how North Korea had not yet set the world on fire. But they seemed entirely blind to all the glaring faults of the political wrecking ball that was Donald J Trump. He was a seeming force of nature who had been enabled by a sycophantic Republican Party held in his thrall.

Who had We the People become and could we return from this ugly borderland? I reached out to my friends and family who shared my concerns. Help me through this crushing disappointment. Tell me we would still recover and heal the festering sores of the political campaign. It had been a shock to discover how many Americans had voted for President Trump. But the final outcome of the election was still frustratingly slow in revealing itself. Had the assault on common decency been rightly repelled?

Looking into the eyes of the body politic was frightening, too many savage ghosts were stirring there. I tried to maintain some semblance of objectivity. "Surety Brings Ruin." I recalled that ancient warning on Apollo's temple to reserve judgement, to accept that one's own most cherished beliefs might be proven wrong in the end. Could I be objective and see both sides of the current political arguments? No dice. I had seen far too much already to change my mind. I was entrenched.

There are times when character declares that we must make choices. The philosophical mind is by its nature skeptical and wary of choosing sides in an argument. In this time of national gut checking, the American character was choosing sides in a way not seen since the Civil War, certainly not seen in my already long lifetime. Primal instincts had been aroused, instincts that had so often erupted into the incessant recurrence of warfare.

We had collectively arrived at a place where it was uncertain if sharing your opinion with your neighbor might be dangerous. People whom I had loved for years became estranged. Families were being torn apart. It seemed as if the very wiring of our national psyche had been tampered with.

Were we truly at a precipice now or was this just a stern warning that foundational cracks threatened our precious political edifice? Time would have to tell. I thought of my friend the professor and his lifetime of self-imposed exile, his perspective of staying on the outside looking inward. I knew enough about him to believe he would appreciate the relevant echoes in a poem I had written in 1990 about confronting the frightening realization that each soul contains the capacity for great good and great evil and that the maintenance of one requires the concealment of the other.

These lines had taken on a new relevance though they had been written long before Trump had appeared on my radar. Whether our departing President would take even the most fleeting glimpse into the dimensions of his soul is known only to him, but I wouldn't take that bet.

At that horizon
Where the eye beholds the soul
Narcissus kneels down at the water's edge
And reflects on the depths below
His image once proud is now pierced with wounds

They stare back at him
Gaping in a mask
Suddenly he is naked in the light of day
Without secrets
And he casts his eyes away.

CHAPTER 57

November 7, 2020

THE DAY BRIGHTENED. NEVADA, Arizona, Georgia and especially Pennsylvania, the province of the Quaker William Penn and the liberal founding genius Benjamin Franklin, these corners of the country were falling Biden's way.

The TV networks were maddeningly slow to call a Democratic victory, perhaps trying not to create the emergence of a false stab-in-the-back conspiracy theory about how the news media was throwing the election unfairly to Joe Biden. Such a conspiracy theory might linger for years and could yet ignite armed conflict between partisans.

Tick...tick...tick...the outcome of the election was starting to come into focus. But the legal minefield still needed clearing. With a stacked judiciary including the Supreme Court, Trump would pursue any legal strategy he could concoct in order to invalidate a fair election.

Late in the day Pennsylvania spoke. It declared Biden the winner of its 20 electoral votes and that clinched the presidency, barring a successful legal challenge. Even though millions more votes had been cast nationally for Biden, the battleground states had had moments of razor-thin margins.

Celebration and sorrow broke out across the nation depending on how you saw things and we all waited to hear from Trump. Would he be gracious and concede? It seemed most improbable, but it was up to him to decide. By evening it was clear that Trump was going to hurl legal grenades all around the battleground states.

I knew we were headed for trouble when Fox News broadcast unsubstantiated allegations by the Trump camp of widespread voter fraud and some of the channel's pundits attempted to give life to this lie. The misguided faithful followers were whipped up into a passionate frenzy and violence seemed to be waiting in the wings.

Fox News had long ago become Trump's organ of propaganda. It had not yet committed itself to the proposition that Biden had won. It remained an outlet where key voices claimed Trump was being victimized, always the victim. It was clear to me that if there was any cheating going on it was likely being done by the master of deception himself, Mr. Donald J. I now expected the nation would have to tolerate a barrage of meritless accusations and legal filings.

It seemed to me that Trump's strategy was not to win in court on the merits but only to clog the wheels of the Electoral College and thereby throw the election into the House of Representatives. In that arena, Republican controlled state delegations were in the majority and therefore might yet re-elect the sly and devious Mr. Trump.

It was time to go to sleep. I knew the judicial branch was now the separated power that would need to dispose of any frivolous allegations with dispatch so Biden's victory could be rightly certified by the specified deadline set for the Electoral College. It seemed to me, as I closed my eyes, that time was of the essence.

CHAPTER 58

November 8, 2020

ON SOME STREETS OF America there were demonstrations of joy celebrating the victory of the Democrats and on other streets there were counterdemonstrations proclaiming a stolen election. Trump was doing his best to stir up unrest because it gave oxygen to his drowning grasp on the organs of governance. Covid 19 was exponentially spreading in what appeared to be a vortex of political denial by vast swaths of the US population who continued to contemptuously scorn wearing masks and to socially distance themselves.

The feedback from around the world on Biden's apparent victory depended on who was asked. The liberal democracies generally sighed a great sigh of relief. The other players on the world stage saw it through the prism of their own interests. The ball was rolling but to where was not quite certain. Historical momentum had definitely felt like it had shifted in a fundamental way.

I imagined how it must have felt on VE day for my parent's generation. Any victory was much slimmer today then in those days.

There would be no outburst of universal relief in America. The wheel was still in spin.

CHAPTER 59

The American Nero Plays The Liar
November 12, 2020

THERE COULD BE NO doubt. America was on fire and the Commander-In-Chief was casting about for accelerant to pour on the flames. An amazing and sobering fact was that 70% of polled Republicans were said to believe this sniveling would-be despot and his assertion that the election had been stolen by devious and unscrupulous methods despite overwhelming evidence to the contrary. Even his subservient Attorney General had stated there was no widespread voter fraud.

After all the lies and distortions over the last four years, how could so many people be gullible enough to buy such demonstrably false and self-serving propaganda? Perhaps some adherents didn't really believe it, maybe they thought it would just confuse and neutralize the enemy, that is us, but that it would do the true believers no harm. It was certain that it must be a mixture of factors that could induce such widespread blindness, such a nonchalant reaction to the mortal danger that Trump's behavior posed to the Republic. It seemed that something akin to hypnosis must be at work. How else could you explain it?

I mused about this irony:

Science searched frantically for a biological latch to lock onto the RNA of this damned virus. Stick a minute piece of protein in just the right place and it would reduce the killer to a harmless smoking hulk of its former deadliness. Where was the psychological equivalent to erase this cult of personality? Science will not be the source of such a magic bullet. I think political evolution will be necessary. We must hold our breath until history declares the outcome.

It seemed that some frail and fatal weakness of the human mind and spirit had been revealed by this charlatan. The susceptibility to nonsense by nearly half our people was shocking. He had clothed his lies in the political yearnings of his core base. I doubt he himself had many fixed values that he cherished other than the drive for power and wealth. The cudgel of projection, the attribution to your opponents of your own faults and lethality, was given a virtuoso performance by the man with the bronzer for skin tone.

Eternal vigilance, that was the prescribed antidote for our enduring vulnerability to such destructive forces. Alarms had been sounded. It was well past the time to start applying an antidote, though it was hard to know what that antidote might be if the truth did not cast sufficient light. It seemed to me that courses in critical thinking should be included in every child's education; not what to think but how to think clearly.

The world was drifting, awaiting political clarification. Covid 19 was ravaging the muddled masses on our side of the Atlantic with no clearly organized or effective effort yet in place to combat it. Overseas the winter Coronavirus wave was hitting even the more cautious capitals hard. Tick, tick, tick.

CHAPTER 60

November 14, 2020

I AWOKE TO THE same game on a different day. The "Million MAGA March" was on in DC and there was no shortage of propaganda-intoxicated subjective thinkers ready to share their warped perceptions of reality with me via interviews on the TV news media. They had answers for everything with their presentation of alternative facts. How was it possible to have a reasoned discussion in such a poisoned atmosphere? This was the kind of brew that Trump thrived in and diligently nurtured. It reminded me of a playful verse I had written some years ago:

THE TORTOISE AND THE HARE

Knowledge and Truth went at it
Knowledge had all the guns
And clearly it had seemed at first
That Knowledge had surely won
But keep an open mind on this

For when it's all said and done
Truth will still be as it is
Though what we knew be gone

CHAPTER 61

November 25, 2020

OVER THE LAST FEW days, Trump's grip on the presidency is loosening. His plan continues to appear to be to delay and obfuscate the Electoral College's task and thus throw the process into the House of Representatives. This effort appeared to be rocked by a few potentially fight- ending body blows.

Pennsylvania and Michigan have certified their votes as did Arizona and Georgia, all won by Joe Biden. A third recount in Georgia is underway but expected to confirm again that Biden has taken that state. Wisconsin has a recount underway but no change in outcome is expected there as well.

Trump is joining the Giuliani circus by telephone today at a meeting with Pennsylvania Republican state legislators but it seems unlikely that Biden's large plurality in that state can be overcome with legal maneuvering through that political body.

CHAPTER 62

November 27, 2020

THE TOP IRANIAN ATOMIC scientist was assassinated in Iran itself today. The timing was impressive. It was conveniently performed before it could land on President Biden's desk as his problem. I would think the Israelis did not want a second opinion on the morality of such a strike. The nuclear bomb maker should have stayed home. His timing was terrible.

More baseless legal moves are afoot by the Trump team in their attempt to get something, anything, in front of a Supreme Court packed with Trump appointees. Tick, tick, tick.

CHAPTER 63

December 8, 2020

It seems ironic that the day after Pearl Harbor Day we have Safe Harbor Day. Today the states reached their deadline to oppose the slate of Electors chosen by the voters. The US Supreme Court refused to hear challenges from the Pennsylvania State Republicans. No other significant legal challenges appeared open to the Naked Emperor. It was time to call off the code blue for his campaign and let it die in peace. Would he continue to pound the chest of his political corpse lying lifeless on the gurney or would he drag the carcass off to some cave and continue to try to revive his political gravy train for another grab at the helm? Stay tuned.

CHAPTER 64

December 11, 2020

HE HAS DRAGGED IT off to his cave. But he is not alone. 18 states' Attorneys General have joined his fruitless search to overthrow a fair election loss. Ted Cruz, that self-proclaimed champion of the Constitution, is apparently prepared to argue this nonsense before the Supreme Court. Is there to be no end to the Republican Party's self-degradation serving this destructive dynamo? Wait...late breaking news...the Supreme Court has refused to hear this legal travesty.

The country is facing a cold winter of hunger and homelessness in the midst of the pandemic while the Emperor throws elaborate holiday bashes without masks at the White House. This is looking more and more like a scene out of Doctor Zhivago; the fortunate aristocrats celebrating the holiday season in an opulent setting while the freezing masses march in the streets seeking bread.

Thankfully, the Covid 19 vaccine was approved today, a remarkably speedy triumph for science. We can now begin to see the end of the pandemic on the horizon and an end to the need for ongoing monetary aid packages. And a stimulus relief bill is under negotiation currently and perhaps that will be the last. There is profound value in preserving our economic infrastructure, keeping small businesses alive and supporting the needy. I am grateful to Congress for their bipartisan efforts in this regard.

CHAPTER 65

December 14, 2020

THE ELECTORAL COLLEGE HAS voted today. It was a good day for democracy. The will of the People was respected despite the avaricious hands of the Biggest Loser. 306 to 232, it wasn't even close despite all the whining and gnashing of teeth. At least a majority of my countrymen had proclaimed with their votes the desire to move beyond this political toxicity and reestablish our enshrined democratic traditions. For that I was grateful and proud

It was time for him to give up the ghost but that never motivated him before.

If punishment should fit the crime, then the loss of freedom and the imposition of powerlessness would make a fitting penalty to address Trump's criminal past. The Southern District of New York was looking into that fairytale ending. The new orange. He always liked orange. That would be a good look.

The first doses of the Covid 19 vaccine were administered in America today while we passed the threshold of 300,000 lost American lives. Now that was hopeful news for a weary nation.

CHAPTER 66

Henry
December 16, 2020

I GOT THE NEWS today from my dear old friend Henry. He was flown back from Guadalajara to Los Angeles via a Mercy Flight. He is on a ventilator now, infected with Covid 19. Henry was like a brother from another mother to me. He had transferred from Guadalajara to New Jersey Med School and we graduated together in the same class from its hallowed halls.

Henry is a down to earth guy, no bullshit except when appropriate to enliven the moment. He loves a good laugh and a good toke at the proper time. Of course, he always had to apply cologne heavily to disguise the telltale evidence when we snuck out for some fun. He had become a very successful Urologist and lived in one of the most exclusive enclaves surrounding San Francisco, truly a dream location. Lisa and I were always happy for him and his wonderful wife, the perfect hostess, Maria.

He had met her at a post office in Guadalajara in the old days, her father was a physician down there. They had forged a long life together with two beautiful daughters and a handsome son. From those humble beginnings a new generation of physicians and grand-children was already springing.

He had a place around Lake Chapala in the countryside outside of Guadalajara. He and Maria had lots of family around. Lisa and I had planned to visit them down there after the pestilence had passed.

Henry's short note was heart wrenching, it said :

"Pray for me."

We are praying for you my friend, every day for your dear soul. May we be together again in laughter.

CHAPTER 67

December 21, 2020

IS IT POSSIBLE THAT the President is hearing about declaring martial law and forcing new elections in the battleground states? Is that affront to our democracy being discussed in the Oval Office, in the People's house? I think so. That is what the news is reporting.

They are saying that this is being proposed by the disgraced General Flynn. It may not be true but if it is I am hoping this is nothing more than the launching of a trial balloon, just the floating of an idea that is frightening yet ultimately recognized as absurd. How dare Trump defile his office with this kind of conversation and conjecture.

On the Congressional front, the Ladies and Gentlemen of both chambers have today passed a Covid stimulus bill but dollars will not arrive in most homes by Christmas since we still await the signature of the President and he is dragging his feet.

This is very poor political theater and it offends a romantic people such as ours. The withholding of relief on the eve of Christmas is an assault on our folk mythology and it is a careless mistake. Something should have been done before the great holiday of giving and cheer. There are shades of *A Christmas Carol* afoot. People are truly starving in huge numbers on the doorstep of the blessed holiday. Jacob Marley, with his rattling chains, should remind us of the power of this season.

There was one very bright Christmas Star in the night sky this evening...Henry was off the ventilator!

Thank You Lord.

CHAPTER 68

December 22, 2020

HOSPITAL WARDS WERE OVERFLOWING across the country and so many lives were holding on by a thread against the killer virus. Emergencies like heart attacks, strokes and trauma cases were being dangerously diverted as hospital beds filled with Covid cases, particularly the ICU's.

Finally, the vaccine was reaching the frontline healthcare workers who had never had a sufficient arsenal of personal protective equipment. They would be safer now, but their ranks were limited in number. They were only human. They were beginning to be overwhelmed again like New York had been last Spring. But the complete outrunning of resources was still a scattered phenomenon, at least so far. Would the entire country be so engulfed that most places would be short of staff and beds? In such chaos, patients would surely die of neglect due to the strain caused by the sheer numbers of the desperately ill.

Up until now I had been hunkered down like a reasonable 71-year-old. Now the vaccine for my risk group was on the horizon.

I had been isolated for nine months already. Would I be able to join the ranks again, be called out of retirement to jump into the mortal struggle because the frontline ranks had become so thin?

For now, I would keep an eye on my community and my state. I would consider the local needs and weigh my options. I would be wise to wait for vaccination before I joined the fight. I do believe the brave men and women out there now would be sufficient to keep the dam from bursting but it was by no means a given.

I so admire all the first responders, the firemen, the police, the medical personnel, the soldiers. One has to love people willing to perform such heroics as they rush headfirst into the breach.

When the flames have lapped at the borders of your home but are beaten back by weary firefighters you had never known personally, you want to kiss that stranger wearing the rubber boots and the funny hat. You may have to experience this yourself to appreciate the poignance of the cleansing tears it evokes. It happened to me more than once in the fire prone hills of southern California.

And late tonight Trump finally spoke up about the coronavirus relief package that Congress had cobbled together so late in the metaphorical day. His contribution to the nation's health: $600 was too small for his deserving citizens. He just might not sign a thing unless it was raised to $2,000 a person. Never mind that Congress was adjourning for Christmas and nothing at all might get done in time for the holiday if he didn't sign the bill on his desk.

He was just that generous a guy. Bah, Humbug.

CHAPTER 69

A Child Was Born Today
In Bethlehem
December 25, 2020

CHRISTMAS DAY AND THE President is in Florida playing golf. He is, no doubt, feeling sorry for himself. The Coronavirus relief bill is sitting on his desk awaiting his signature while millions of Americans face starvation and eviction. The defense budget has been vetoed for the first time in almost 60 years.

It seems clear to me that Trump intends to make the country suffer for its rejection of his criminal enterprise and that the corrupt pardons that are flowing out of his office in bulk are additional icing on his reprehensible cake. The fact that he has not condemned Russia for its recent massive security breach of our institutional cyberspace again raises the question: what motivates him to coddle our opponents so consistently to the detriment of his own nation?

CHAPTER 70

December 27, 2020

SOLOMON AND PONTIUS PILATE were both men of power and arbiters of the law. There is a long and varied line of such embodiments. Emperor Donald, in his Florida colosseum, slowly indicates a thumbs up on the Coronavirus relief and spending bill. This averts a government shutdown amid all the chaos already swirling. It was very close to the deadline. The odd timing is of his own choosing. This dramatic gesture is dropped on Sunday night in the symbolic dead space between Christmas and New Year's Eve. The anticlimax is deafening and the crowd seems oddly quiet.

It seemed to me to be the cry of a dying swan
Who hopes to be a phoenix.
There is much unfinished business
As danger continues to hover
Above our stricken land.

CHAPTER 71

A Bright Morning Shattered
By Insurrection
January 6, 2021

GEORGIA HAD SPOKEN TODAY. The Senate will have a Democratic majority. The gavel at the Senate has been pried loose from the death grip of the Grim Reaper from Kentucky. Here is a bright ray of national renewal. I am thankful for my country. The opportunity for a coordinated effort to cope with the myriad challenges before us is coming into focus. The fever may have broken but the patient remains in critical condition. Will the spell be broken as the Great Dissembler, that rough beast, slouches toward Mar-a-Lago to bemoan?

That was this morning and then the riot breached the Capitol building itself and the Congress sheltered in place. Thankfully no mass shooting broke out. We could be relieved that there were not more casualties than actually occurred. Restraint on the side of the police obviously kept insurgent dead to a minimum. Still the mayhem, injury, death and defilement of our Capitol was a deep shock to the Nation.

The Capitol police force struggled mightily to protect the Joint Session of Congress in the face of the overwhelming assault of the crowd. It was not clear why adequate additional Federal forces were not deployed in a timely fashion to control the mob. The inquiry into these events has just begun but suspicious eyes were cast toward the President. After all, it was he who summoned his followers to descend on Washington DC on that date. He and his surrogates had been urging resistance to the "steal" for months and had whipped up the crowd just prior to their violent attack on the Capitol Building as Congress was performing a most solemn function of certifying the Election result. The disgraceful delay in deploying the National Guard must be attributed to the Commander-in-Chief who reportedly watched the rampage for hours on TV without taking steps to contain it. The day took on the look of an aborted coup d'état rather than a spontaneous riot of disappointed Trump supporters.

During the night, after the halls of the Capitol had been cleared of marauders, Congress did assert its authority and certified the Biden ticket. It did so over the shameful efforts of many members of Congress who persisted in challenging the validity of the valid election despite the absence of any compelling evidence to the contrary and despite the freshly tragic episode of sedition that had grown out of the flames they themselves had fanned.

It appeared that the coup attempt had failed, but the millions of passionate partisans backing Trump remained incensed. Danger and uncertainty hovered. These events had set the whole world on edge.

CHAPTER 72

A Day Of Pride, A Day Of Shame
January 13, 2021

THE HOUSE OF REPRESENTATIVES voted to impeach the would-be Napoleon, yet nearly 200 of his sycophants voted against the measure. After cowering for their lives, the spell still had not broken for these misguided souls. Even the figurative confinement of Trump to his Palm Beach Elba seemed unfitting to these short-sighted functionaries.

The Lord had asked for ten good men as the price to spare Sodom and Gomorrah. Ten showed up today from the Republican caucus and joined the House Democrats in voting for impeachment. There was one from Myrtle Beach, South Carolina. I am grateful to him. He described himself as a loyal supporter of the President through thick and thin. But his short walk on the road to Damascus last week had shaken off the scales from his eyes.

I am allowed to fumble in my mind as I sit in my home. I can ramble and have offensive points of view but I am not in that House.

Not before the eyes of history. Patrick Henry's cry of "give me liberty or give me death" still rings with forceful passion today because it was real, it was heroic. The oratory I saw today in the House and Senate in support of the insurgent President was not descended from Mr. Henry, it was more like Josef Goebbels in a duet with Neville Chamberlain sounding out a chorus of lies and appeasement. And above all this din, there is the quiet resolve of the seasoned Mr. Biden, his thumb decidedly not on the scale. Let us pray.

CHAPTER 73

It Is Snowing In DC
January 15, 2021

I AM WATCHING TV news and there is snowfall in DC. The reporter is standing in an empty urban landscape reporting that 20,000 troops will be deployed in the city by inauguration day. Other deployments are expected around several state capitals.

That would be cause enough for worry but we await the arrival of our fifth grandchild any day now and Lisa and I are quarantining so that we can visit. We are nervous of course. My beautiful daughter Bailey is such a good mother. I have told her since she was a child that I knew how good a mother she would be someday. She is such an intelligent, funny and good-natured human being. Don't get me started on how wonderful a human being and mother my daughter Viena is, another beautiful lady inside and out. Both are so creative and concerned about the human and natural world around them. They get that from their mother, we all get that from their mother.

This will be a child welcomed into a home illuminated by thought, humor and love.

CHAPTER 74

Aftermath
January 20, 2021

PRESIDENT BIDEN AND VICE President Harris were inaugurated with all the dignified but attenuated pomp that the besieged Capital could safely provide. Their supporters rejoiced and many millions of Trump supporters mourned fearing the descent into the demon territory of socialism that they were sure was bound to follow.

To me it was clear that our democracy had dodged a bullet...just. There would still be time to tend to the wounds of our divisions, if only there were a consensus for healing.

Thus ended this phase of battle in the American Cold Civil War but the danger was far from over. Trump had a huge war chest and over 74,000,000 sympathetic ears to continue to mislead. To be sure the world would watch and wait. Perhaps in time his cult of personality would fade and it would become another Lost Cause that the country would have to try to digest. Hopefully we would overcome the political ravages of this national torment but that remained to be determined. Political Reconstruction would have to occur. Reconstitution might be a better description.

President Biden would have an opportunity for greatness. He might yet wear the mantle of a Lincoln. "With malice toward none, with charity toward all" as the great man had said. Let us hope our nation will remember those famous words and that this frail 78-year-old President is able to fulfill his promise, to bind up the nation's wounds.

And my family? We would all survive, God willing, though there would be challenges ahead.

Unlike Zhivago, I would likely not lose all my most cherished loved ones in a whirlwind of chaos. With good fortune we would all get past the pandemic and the dangers of political upheaval and we would all meet our timely and natural ends as befits those who have lived well.

The paucity of power we have to alter events comes into its sharpest focus when epochs rise and fall. With the exception of the Cuban Missile Crisis, not until this late time in my life did the hinge of fate swing so ominously toward the abyss. This brush with danger must serve to remind us just how vulnerable our democracy and liberty really are. We fall asleep again at our own peril.

Eternal vigilance, as they say, is the price of collective freedom, but each of us is the guardian of our own soul.

> We are all bound to the same burning sea
> Abundant in islands of safety
> And he who believes that harm is asleep
> May awake to the terror of danger
> That his are the eyes that narrow with fear

When his home and his flesh are invaded
A dream is secure for only so long
As the din of the battle has faded.

CHAPTER 75

Recovery

I WANT TO ADDRESS all my fellow countrymen, not just those who agree with me.

This torrent we have endured has strained and torn at the bonds of love and family. People we have cherished seem distant and guided by principles we now find abhorrent. Reason no longer seems capable of bridging the gaps of political belief between friends, neighbors and relatives to whom we once felt so close. I am reminded of Generals Lewis Armistead and Winfield Hancock, opposing officers at Pickett's charge at Gettysburg. They were both severely wounded quite close to each other on Cemetery Ridge....enemies, yet each asking about the other's wellbeing after the battle. The bonds of their long friendship had not been eclipsed by the enmity of war.

I welcome all those whose spirits touched mine before this chasm opened. I hope to see the affection rekindle where darkness has descended. It will require mutual effort and understanding but the alternative will lead to persistent division. May healing impulses arise from the grass roots for that is where we live. We must learn to overcome fear and lies, for those are the weapons that tyrants will wield to assault our domestic tranquility.

CHAPTER 76

Further

January 23, 2021

LITTLE LORELEI CECILIA SHOONER, our fifth grandchild, was born healthy with her mother safe and her father Peter beaming on the night of January 22, 2021. There were signs that welcomed her. She was born with a true knot in her umbilical cord during a power outage in the freezing Ohio winter on her dear departed Grandfather Matthew's birthday bearing his bright blue eyes in the midst of a pandemic. The ancient Greeks would have found this all very interesting. I am just thankful to the universe that has given us all life.

The knotted cord was an incidental finding. It was only recognized after her birth. Without warning it could easily have been fatal to sweet little Lorelei. Our tightly knit family world was so nearly struck by a devastating asteroid....and we had never seen it coming.

I awoke happily from a dream this morning. I had escaped pursuit from a resort island on a rubber dinghy with a powerful engine in a driving rainstorm. When I left my bed I stepped outside to a sunny and crisp South Carolina winter's day. I was still warm in my heavy shirt. My beloved Lisa sat beside me on our porch watching the dog run happily in search of his ball while we drank our steaming coffee. If you haven't experienced a low country morning like this, you're really missing something brilliant and beautiful.

CHAPTER 77

Exeunt

I LEAVE THIS STORY at a vital juncture. Life itself will write the ending and the conclusion will be clear enough to all. Though this age seems confused, in the end the resolution of our present difficulties, one way or the other, is not likely to be ambiguous.

Prophets of doom may then appear to have been overdramatic but this is merely a quirk of timing.

It is likely that in the long future ahead there will indeed come times of desperate dislocation. A time when dreamers will be necessary to remind us of the potential for beauty in this world and of all the fruits that come from its pursuit,

Dreamers like Yuri Zhivago.

And so, I end as I began:

Becoming Zhivago is a lifelong endeavor. You must be prepared to endure the hardships that the cycles of nature and the depredations of mankind may inflict. And, if the tempest rages, should you fall, stand up again. Stand up always for human dignity as best you can.

Take into the world your own vision of the glory of creation.

In the midst of danger when survival is threatened, the search for meaning and purpose, the struggle to maintain a life affirming morality, these efforts may seem to be the mere strivings of dreamers and detached theologians. But it is also the province of philosophers and poets.

That is where the beacon leads. That is where the driven soul can find shelter and inspiration while chaos swirls all about.

That is the territory I would hope to always inhabit.

SECTION TWO

FIGURES OF SPEECH AND
THE BEARERS OF BEING

POETRY HAS THE CAPACITY to maximize aesthetic and intellectual content while permitting an economy of words. It invites a profusion of metaphors, images and symbols. The book of poems that follows is a means of relating one psychic journey through our time and place, an arena to allow ideas, values and emotions that were formed there to play out on a stage.

Poetry can be more incisive than prose. It can dive into crevices that are otherwise elusive. It is its very directness that attracts me. It aims at a certain purity that is hard to achieve with prose. For me, it is a sharper instrument to use in the attempt to describe the indescribable. That is no small advantage.

But reading someone else's poetry can be an arduous and frustrating challenge for it often approaches the ring of an incomprehensible foreign language. If made understandable and found to be relatable, poetry can move the mind and emotion in ways that approach the sublime. I hope these offerings will be comprehensible and edifying. That was my intention in their writing.

I would suggest when reading Section Two to select a topic which interests you. There are poems that are grouped together by theme and you will find many different levels of intensity and complexity with some approaching simplicity. Feel free to contact me if you need clarification or if you wish to discuss the work. The email address to send comments and questions to is at the website below.

SECTION TWO CAN BE ACCESSED FOR FREE ONLINE
AT: bearersofbeing.com

IMAGE ATTRIBUTIONS

Milton Keynes UK
Ingram Content Group UK Ltd.
UKHW051039140923
428659UK00010B/70

9 798822 904682